To Lucy
Love

Tristram Shandy Uncovered

George Marshall

© George Marshall 2015

All rights reserved

No part of this publication may be reproduced, stored in a retrieval system, or transmitted in any form or by any means, without the prior permission in writing of the publisher, nor be otherwise circulated in any form of binding or cover other than that in which it is published and without a similar condition including this condition being imposed on the subsequent purchaser.

All paper used in the printing of this book has been made from wood grown in managed, sustainable forests.

ISBN: 978-1-78003-873-5

Printed and published in the UK

Author Essentials Ltd
Sussex House
190 South Coast Road
Peacehaven
East Sussex
BN10 8JJ

A catalogue record of this book is available from the British Library

Cover design by Jacqueline Abromeit

By the same author:

Earth Cell
The Accrington Folly
The Earth Party
The Grey Tractor
Life With An Invented Father
The Shadow of Innocence

1

The wooden panelling, so solid in appearance, fell away from the wall with little pressure from Alan's pry bar. Dust from years of woodworm life rose up into his nostrils. The whole panelling would have to come off; his dream of having a cottage in the North Yorkshire countryside was becoming an expensive nightmare. He pressed on with this dispiriting task and down with the next worm-eaten panel came a bundle of papers. They were tied tightly in a bow, and when he blew off the dust Alan saw, written on the cover in large faded copperplate, *The Corporal's Story*. His heart quickened—was this valuable? An original manuscript by a famous author? He rubbed his roughened hands on his jeans, and carefully undid the bow. Pages of neat handwriting were revealed, the ink brown with age. Alan had not heard of *James Butler*, the name on the cover, but that meant nothing, the few books he read were mainly contemporary action-packed accounts by former military men. He carefully re-tied the bow; if the cottage had a history Wendy might be more interested in living there.

He arrived back late at the flat, tired after a long day's work, and with little appetite for the supper Wendy had kept warm for him.

'I ate mine before it was spoilt,' she said.

'It's fine,' he said.

'That place is taking up all your time—and your money.'

'I've brought something that will interest you.'

'What is it?'

'In that plastic bag by the door.'

'Where did you find these papers?' she said, returning with the opened bundle.

'In the cottage—they were behind a panel.' He said nothing about having to remove the infested woodwork. 'I thought you would want to read them.'

'I'm not in a mood for anything to do with the cottage,' her voice hardened.

'This could be a valuable historical document,' he persisted.

'You read it then.'

'I'm too whacked tonight.'

Alan had been with Wendy less than a year when he bought the cottage. Paid for from the compensation he got for his injuries in the gas-rig explosion. They had met on a cruise to the Norwegian fiords from Hull. With him was his former workmate, Terry, whose idea it was to go on the cruise. 'How do you fancy going on the North Sea again—this time on a cruise liner?' he said, when they were having a pint together. Terry had also been injured in the gas-rig accident, his injuries more severe, and he still walked with a stick. Stuck on the static rig, Alan had often stared out at passing boats, wishing he too was moving towards a different destination. He fancied the prospect of steaming past some rig and watching guys grafting and going nowhere. But all he actually saw from the cruise ship were lights in the night and the glow from the flaring-off.

Wendy was on the cruise with Maureen, a married woman who worked with her at the wool shop. Maureen was keen to go on a cruise, and had persuaded Wendy to accompany her. Wendy had no particular wish for a cruise, or to see the Norwegian fiords, but she hadn't had a proper holiday in the years since her divorce. A guided tour of stately homes in England would be her first choice, if she'd had a friend to go with. It quickly became clear to her that the main attraction of the cruise for Maureen, was the opportunity for sexual encounters in the compressed social atmosphere of on-board life.

At dinner on the second evening they shared a table with Terry and Alan. The two men assailed by the aroma of Maureen's perfume, her wide eyes brimming with desire. Terry, plainly excited by Maureen's unmistakeable availability, suggested they all went for a drink. Wendy, who had not come on the cruise seeking sex, became alarmed by what was developing, and went with Maureen to the ladies toilet to make her thoughts known.

'I fancy that Maureen,' Terry said, when the two women were away.

'Me too,' said Alan. Maureen was the dark-haired, busty type of woman he was attracted to. The other, the slim blondish one, had the pale blue eyes which in his mind were associated with a cold nature.

'We'll have to toss a coin,' said Terry.

'Let's wait until we hear what the girls have to say.'

In the ladies toilet, Maureen, forceful and persuasive, was working on Wendy, seeking to overcome her companion's reluctance to be involved in a pairing. Unused to much alcohol, the effect of the several cocktails Wendy had drunk began to tell, dissolving her resistance. 'Not the fat one,' she said, the toilet light gyrating above her.

'Oh...' said Maureen, disappointed.

'The dark one... black curly hair... brown, brown eyes...'

'Alan?—are you sure?'

'The other one... like... like my ex-husband...'

'Alright then, I'll tell Terry I'll go with him.'

2

Wendy waited nervously in the cabin she shared with Maureen, who'd departed eagerly for the men's cabin. She'd had a couple more cocktails to help her face the oncoming encounter, and felt quite tipsy. Her heart, already beating fast, quickened further when the knock came to the cabin door. She had difficulty in getting up from the chair, her hand unsure as she turned the door handle.

'I haven't done it for years,' she blurted out, as soon as the door closed.

'And you don't have to do it now, love,' Alan said.

'I'm sorry…'

'I've brought us something to drink,' he said, and sat down.

She didn't want any more alcohol, but took some comfort from his considerate attitude. Her eyes never left him as he took the other chair and flipped opened a can. She saw nothing to fear in the dark brown eyes looking back at her, and in the confined cabin his close male presence stirred in her a dormant desire for sex. If she were ever going to be with a man again there would be no better time to start than this. Resolved, unsteady on her feet, she took off her dress and lay down in the bottom bunk, rigid with expectation. He joined her and she tried to relax.

He was gone when she woke—she had been a disappointment, the thought crushing. She heard movement above and Alan got down from the other bunk.

'I thought you had left me,' she said.

'These bunks aren't big enough for two—anyway not for sleeping,' he said, bending over and giving her a kiss. 'Are we alright for tonight?' asked the first man she had been with since her divorce.

'Yes,' she said, which was slight expression of the joy she felt.

The next night she was much more relaxed, and with their bodies in tight embrace room for Alan to sleep with her in the narrow bunk.

'How're you getting on with your little blonde?' Terry asked, the two of them having a drink together.

'Fine,' he said. 'Good,' he added, prompted by an unusual feeling of protectiveness, and not wishing to give any suggestion of Wendy's restrained sexual response.

'Maureen fancies you and she's talking about swapping partners for tonight. I told her you'd be up for it, you wanting her at the start. I don't mind a change for one night—be your chance with the sexy Maureen.'

Alan was silent, it was true what Terry said, and he was tempted. 'I'll see what Wendy thinks,' a reply which surprised Terry.

He found Wendy out on the deck alone, gazing up at the towering sides of the fiord.

'Majestic,' he said, 'that's what the booklet says.'

'I feel so tiny—even the boat's small against these cliffs.'

He told her what was being suggested.

'It was Maureen you wanted,' she said, looking scared.

'I know you now,' he said.

'Everything's so unreal on a boat,' a glitter of tears in her blue eyes.

'I'll say no to a swap—unless you'd like a change?'

She shook her head.

He stayed with her for a while, the boat moving slowly along the fiord, neither saying much.

'Purely a ship-board romance,' Maureen, with her husband waiting, told Wendy at the end of the cruise. But Wendy, revived by this renewed experience of male company, had already agreed to meet Alan back in York.

A cold drizzle fell out of the night sky as, shivery and apprehensive, Wendy approached the wine-bar where they were to meet. Although little more than a week since coming ashore, life on the cruise liner had become a distant dream-like world. Would Alan even be here? She had herself been uncertain about coming. It had taken an act of will to leave the cosy security of her flat, and come alone to this downtown bar. From the doorway her eyes searched the lively bar, but she couldn't see Alan amongst this merry-sounding assembly. Beneath the sharp hurt of rejection, was a feeling of relief that the enflamed plans made on the boat were over, and no more would be expected of her.

'Wendy—over here,' Alan stood up at a table.

'I'm sorry I'm late,' she said, dropping onto a chair, not waiting for any embrace.

'I'm glad you decided to come,' he said.

This was the man she knew, and she began to warm to his smile. She slipped off her damp coat, and Alan went to get her a coffee. At first they talked about the cruise, reminiscing about this, their only shared experience. Their talk petered out, and the question of what next, hung in the air. 'I'd be ashamed to take you back to my grotty place,' Alan said, breaking the silence. He had lived in a rented room since his relationship with a single mother came apart several months ago. 'My flat's not far from here,' said Wendy. With Alan by her side the night was no longer scary. He stayed the night. 'Next week come for a meal,' she said, with a feeling of having landed safely ashore.

The night spent with Wendy became a regular weekly arrangement, a night Alan looked forward to with pleasure. He didn't like living alone, and would still have been with the single mother if he'd been able to put up with the uncontrolled behaviour of her three young children. His attempt to intervene in their management had been a complete failure, having little effect on the children, causing the resentment of the mother, and him moving out. Each time he returned from the comfort and companionship of being with Wendy, to the cold silence of his dismal room, his spirits sank. Alan's comments about his dire accommodation left no doubt in Wendy's mind that he would jump at the chance to move in with her. Denying the urgings of her body, she held back from inviting him more often, not wishing to encourage him into thinking that he could move in with her. At the time of her divorce she had resolved never to put herself within the control of a man again. Though now, with fifty on the horizon and the cheerless prospect of ageing alone, the temptation to take a risk with Alan was strong. But was he only interested in getting somewhere better than his rented room?

He began to stay overnight at the flat two nights in the week, an arrangement which seemed to come about by unspoken agreement. He offered to make the meal on one of the nights, but Wendy wouldn't let him do any cooking. He thought it odd that she was willing to share her bed with him, but not her stove. 'I couldn't have allowed you to take over my kitchen,' she later told him. Soon he was spending almost half the week at the flat, Wendy, acquiescing to this development and avoiding having to make a decision. A direct proposal to share her home would have burdened her by thoughts of the risks involved, and brought a resurgence of bruising memories of her marriage. She would likely have refused, yet, almost imperceptibly, it happened, and within six months of leaving the boat, Alan was living at the flat full-time.

He felt properly established the first time he made their evening meal, access to the stove finally granted. Though it was a shock for Wendy the first time she came into the kitchen and saw Alan at the stove, memories of her dominating ex-husband welling up. What had she done—risking all that again? But with a man in her life she felt more like a proper woman, and her fears of a lonely future were held at bay. Alan, though of a similar age, gave little thought to the future. Fit and healthy, he still felt young, the limp from his injuries in the explosion barely noticeable. He smoked only an occasional roll-up, and was normally not much of a drinker; he despised his contemporaries with their fat guts and ailments.

He had led an unsettled life, the vagaries and uncertainties of the building trade bringing little constancy. He'd lived with a number of women, though none of the relationships had led to the altar. Life with Wendy gave a settled regularity which he had not previously experienced. Sometimes, when he looked at her as they sat at the table, or watched television, Alan imagined her as a sister.

3

Wendy was happy with the way that living with Alan was working out, and he felt content with the arrangement. Then he bought the cottage. It had been his ambition to have his own place, an ambition that had intensified during his years as a jobbing builder, living in lodgings and rented rooms, whilst working on the houses of home-owners. More than a desire to possess a building and a patch of land, it was a wish to have the stability and contentment he believed went along with owning your own home. He said nothing to Wendy about his intention to buy a place, hoping to surprise her when he'd found somewhere. The cottage, although in need of renovation, had a sizeable area of garden, and was just the thing for a builder able to do all the work himself.

'I'm buying a house,' Alan announced as he came into the flat, his eyes shining, unable to contain his delight. Wendy, standing at the stove, turned to him, a frown clouding her face.

'A house…? I don't understand,' she said, nervously.

'A cottage—'

'Are you leaving me…?' her voice faltered, her hands gripping the edge of the kitchen table. She stared at him in disbelief.

'A house for us—a cottage in the country—with a garden.'

'I never expected this,' she sat down.

'I wanted it to be a surprise. I've got the keys from the agent—we can go and look at it today. I have to make a decision.'

'Out in the country,' she murmured, her face troubled.

She was silent in the pickup as they drove out of town, conscious of the passing miles taking her away from her home in the city. They came into a village where there was little sign of life on this cold, grey day. Alan stopped in front of a house which had an abandoned look, boards covering a couple of the windows. He jumped out, a bunch of keys in his hand, and strode up to the door. He swung open the old wooden door and Wendy followed him into the house. She shivered in the damp and chilling air. There were a few remnants of furniture, and some mouldering carpets. Dust lay everywhere. They went through the house together, Alan enthusiastic in describing the work he would do, telling her of the improvements he would make.

'For a builder this place is a bargain,' he said, 'I'll never get another chance like this.'

'What will I do out here?—we must have come twenty miles.'

'More like fifteen.' But fifteen or fifty, he was in reach of achieving his ambition, a few miles was not going to stand in his way.

'I'm happy where I am,' she said.

'You'll love it here when it's all finished,' he said, his decision made.

The sale was completed, and for the first time in his life Alan owned a piece of the land of his birth. Full of pride he informed Wendy, but her reaction to this historic event was not what he had hoped for, her pale blue eyes regarding him coldly. He realised then that, in addition to the work on the cottage, he was also faced with the task of persuading Wendy of the advantages to living there. This would not be easy, she seemed set against leaving her flat and moving out into the country, unwilling to discuss, or even mention the cottage. Yet its presence was a constant source of tension between them. Her warmth cooled and sex, never significant in their friendship, became almost non-existent. Alan was so persuaded himself of the advantages of living at the cottage, that he didn't give up hope of Wendy coming round to the idea of moving there. He remained determined to fulfil his ambition of living in a home that he owned, yet did not want to be faced with having to decide between the cottage and Wendy. But the possibility of life without her had crept into his mind.

Working alone all day at the cottage, with the prospect of an evening eating a meal in almost total silence, and expecting only sleep in bed, his thoughts drifted to other, more enticing, possibilities. If they were going to split, what was stopping him now from brightening up his life? An image of the abundant and sexual Maureen teased his imagination. She fancies you, Terry had said. But he made no move, either with regard to Maureen or any woman. Life with Wendy had become a habit, a settled place where he was comfortably housed and fed, and able to continue work on the cottage. It would be foolish to risk upsetting things, and it would end any prospect of Wendy and him continuing together. She had become so much part of his life, and he held to the belief that it was only a matter of time before their close friendship resumed. He wondered how he could help to bring it about. What if he offered to marry her?

Alan had now been working on the cottage for over six months and the money was running out. Renovation was costing more than he had estimated, his work exposing defects in the building he hadn't reckoned on. Although Wendy had said nothing to suggest that she had changed her mind, in his desperation Alan convinced himself that she had become more accepting of the cottage, and he decided to sound her out about the possibility of a loan. He thought this might be the time to bring up the question of marriage. He didn't know if she had any money but knew there was no mortgage on the flat, bought with the settlement from her divorce, Wendy's childless twenty-year marriage ending when her husband left to live with his pregnant woman friend.

She gave him no time to explain, the mere mention of the cottage and his difficulties released her pent up feelings. 'You went ahead with it as if I didn't exist,' she screamed at him. 'Well you can sort it out yourself.' Wendy, who hardly ever raised her voice, shouting and likely to have been heard by the neighbours, shocked him into silence by this outburst.

'You've only seen it in a broken down state. Wait till you see the cottage when it's finished—the garden all cleared,' he wanted to say, but she stalked off to bed. Why she couldn't see how much better it would be living there than in the stuffy flat, baffled him, leaving Alan convinced that he would never understand women. He sat a while wondering what he could do about the cottage, but came to no clear conclusion and went up to bed.

Expecting an icy reception after their quarrel, her hot embrace was a complete surprise, Wendy not usually the one to take the initiative in bed. No words were exchanged during the intensely passionate sex which followed, or afterwards as they both lay exhausted. Never before had she been so unrestrained, it was as if, Alan thought as he sank into sleep, the heated anger she had shown earlier had released more than her feelings about the cottage. In the morning neither mentioned the previous night, but the smile Wendy gave him dismissed any thoughts he'd had about her being like a sister.

His mind that day as he worked at the cottage was dominated by this changed vision of Wendy, absent now any thoughts of Maureen and of sexual solace elsewhere. When he got back to the flat that evening, the chill in the atmosphere which had existed these past weeks was gone. Wendy had waited for him, and they ate together. Later, when she was busy on her laptop, he turned off the TV, untied the bundle from the cottage, and began to read these discovered pages.

The Corporal's Story

by James Butler

Otherwise titled,
The Life and Sensibilities of James Butler, Corporal

Chapter One

I well remember the day *Tristram Shandy* was born. In his chronicle, *Tristram* goes back further, to the time of his conception. I was begot, he writes, in the night betwixt the first Sunday and the first Monday in the month of March, in the year of our Lord one thousand seven hundred and eighteen. He is able to know the exact date, he says, because his father was a most regular man in everything he did. On the first Sunday of each month, it was Mr *Shandy's* habit to wind up a large house clock which stood on the back stairs. Years later his father, observing the young *Tristram* behaving in ways different to his own, expressed to his brother, *Toby*, a foreboding that his nephew would neither think nor act like any other man's child. He said that his son's misfortunes began nine months before ever he came into the world, and indicated that his wife, in asking during the act of procreation, '*have you not forgot to wind up the clock,*' had caused a damaging interruption.

Tristram speaks of his understanding of the sensitivity of what he refers to as the homunculus, and its vulnerability in the process of conception, believing that his father's mood had adversely affected his future development. He says it scattered and dispersed the animal spirits whose business it was to have escorted and go hand-hand with the homunculus, and conduct him safe to the place destined for his reception. *My little gentleman had got to his journey's end miserably spent,* he writes.

Whatever state he was in when life was initiated, it had taken form and was now on the point of being revealed to the world. Four of us were gathered at *Shandy Hall*, downstairs in the back parlour by the fire, for it was a November day. The Feast of St *Elizabeth*, said Doctor *Slop*, who was of the *Roman* faith, and the only physician in the district. I was there with Captain *Toby Shandy*, known within the family, and among the servants, as Uncle *Toby*. Over the years I had become more than a common servant to Captain *Shandy*, and now his close companion. We had come along to *Shandy Hall* to join the Captain's brother, *Walter Shandy*, in awaiting the arrival of the baby. Mrs *Shandy* upstairs in her bedroom with her personal maid, *Susannah*.

Why do I wish to tell you of an event that has already been described elsewhere in detail, and at considerable length? My name is *James Butler* but known better as corporal *Trim*, for it was in King *William's* army that I first encountered Captain S*handy*, serving in the Captain's own company of foot-soldiers. When, many years later, I read *Tristram Shandy's* account of his life, I felt belittled by his portrayal of the humble corporal. I thanked God that Grandfather *Naylor* was no longer of this world, and spared such a slighting view of his grandson. Enabled now by the legacy from Captain *Shandy* to bear the cost of paper, I am intent upon retaking possession of my own history. But first the birth of the man, who gave an account of his own life which was to produce a parody of mine.

*

Dr *Slop*, a short man, sat slumped in a chair as if pressed down into it by his huge belly. His presence had not originally been anticipated as the midwife had been given charge. There had, I discovered, been opposition from Mr *Shandy* to his wife's desire to have the local midwife, believing, that the delivery of his unborn child should have the benefit of the latest advances in medical science. He was convinced that the child would be safer in the hands of an up to date member of the medical profession, than those of an ageing woman who had delivered babies for many years in the self—same manner.

Over the years I learned a great deal about *Walter Shandy*, much from the Captain, and also from personal experience. A well-educated, widely-read man, Mr *Shandy* kept himself informed of the latest ideas and scientific developments. He was a great believer in hypotheses, of which he had numerous at his disposal for use in dealing with aspects of life that were giving him concern. His hypotheses were created out of his own enquiries, and, fitting his singular manner of thought, were held by Mr *Shandy* alone. Once he had formed and established an hypothesis he would conform, in his behaviour and attitude, to its particular logic.

An aspect of his concern about the delivery of the baby arose from his understanding that all souls were equal at the start, and it was the treatment they were subjected to following conception that determined the character of an individual. The soul, Mr *Shandy* concluded after much research, was located in the cerebellum. He was shocked to discover the incredibly high pressure exerted on the pliable head of a baby during parturition, appalled by the distortion to the soul this could cause. He reasoned that if the child could be turned around and delivered feet first, there would be considerably less damage to the soul. He believed Dr *Slop* would be more open to the idea of turning the child in the womb than would a village midwife fixed in her ways.

Mr *Shandy* searched for a way that a child could be born which would avoid the damaging pressures, which he now decided had been the cause of his first son, *Robert*, born with his head foremost, *turning out afterwards to be a lad of wonderful slow parts*. He looked into the use of *Caesarian* section, and found numerous accounts of men of genius and renown, who, like *Caesar*, had come into the world in this manner. From his readings he was satisfied that incisions into the *abdomen* and *uterus* were not mortal, but the mere factual mention of such a thing had Mrs *Shandy* turn as pale as ashes, which put an end to that possibility.

In spite of all his attempts to persuade her otherwise, Mrs *Shandy* maintained her insistence on having the midwife, a motherly woman of proven reputation, who trusted little to her own efforts and a great deal to those of mother nature. Until six or seven years ago there had been no midwife nearer the parish than six or seven miles long miles riding over muddy roads. The parson's wife decided that her husband's flock deserved better, and involved herself in the appointment of the present midwife, a woman of the parish in her forty-seventh year, of decent carriage and grave deportment, left a widow with four children, and in great distress. The parson's wife, supported by her husband, saw to payment for the necessary licensing. *Tristram* writes thus of the parson:

Be it known then, for five years before the date of the midwife's licence …the parson we have to do with, had made himself a country talk by a breach of all decorum, which he had committed against himself, his station and his office; —and that was, in never appearing better, or otherwise mounted, than on a lean, sorry, jack ass of a horse, value about one pound fifteen shillings; who, to shorten all descriptions of him, was full brother to Rosinante, as far as similitude congenial could make him; for he answered his description to a hair-breadth in everything,—except that I do not remember 'tis anywhere said, that Rosinante was broken winded; and that, moreover, Rosinante, as is the happiness of most Spanish horses, fat or lean,—was undoubtedly a horse of all points… To speak the truth, he never could enter a village, but he caught the attention of both old and young—Labour stood still as he pass'd,—the bucket hung suspended in the middle of the well,— the spinning wheel forgot its round,—even chuck-farthing and shuffle-cap themselves stood gaping till he had got out of sight.

The man on the horse is the young parson *Yorick*, who in later life when I knew him, was, from all accounts little changed in his attitude to the standards of appearance and decorum expected of a churchman. The only *Yorick* I had earlier heard of was *Shakespeare's* dead jester, which made me think our parson was from *Denmark*, but the Captain said *Yorick* could trace his forbears in *England* for hundreds of years, much longer than could the *Shandy* family.

Mrs *Shandy's* real desire was for the birth of her children to be in *London* where facilities were more advanced than out in the country. To be assured of this, her marriage settlement, *between the said Walter Shandy and Elizabeth Mollineux*, had provision for her to be paid £120 should *Walter Shandy* move from *London* to his estate at *Shandy Hall*, and *as often as the said Elizabeth Mollineux shall happen to be enceint with child or children severally and lawfully begot. Walter Shandy* also responsible for defraying any costs incurred beyond £120. The Captain told me that, at his suggestion, a clause was inserted to protect his brother from the possibility of false claims. For this reason Mrs *Shandy* was giving birth at *Shandy Hall* as in September of the year previous, she had gone to *London* for what proved to be a false alarm.

In the coach during the journey back from *London*, her husband complained bitterly of the unnecessary expense of its hire, and of being taken away from *Shandy Hall* at a time when his wall-fruit, greengages especially, were just ready for pulling. He could not understand how his wife came to think she was with child, unable to rid his mind of the possibility of deceit. 'He would have tired out the patience of any flesh alive,' Mrs *Shandy* told the Captain. In spite of her pleas, Mr *Shandy* had insisted she forfeit the right to a second payment; what she was unwilling to give up was the right to choose who should attend on her at the birth.

'How does your mistress?' Mr *Shandy*, coming into the parlour, enquired of the passing *Susannah*.

'As well as can be expected,' she said, without pausing on her way to the stairs.

'What a fool I am, brother *Toby*, 'tis ever the precise answer. Of all the riddles of married life—of all the puzzling riddles in the married state, of which you may trust me, brother, there are many, there is not one that has more intricacies in it than this. That from the very moment the mistress of the house is brought to bed, every female in it, from my lady's gentlewoman down to the cinder-wench, becomes an inch taller for it; and give themselves more airs upon that single inch, than their other inches put together.'

'I think,' said the Captain, 'that 'tis we sink an inch lower. If I but meet a woman with child—I do it. 'Tis a heavy tax upon that half of our fellow creatures, brother *Shandy*—'tis a piteous burden on them,' shaking his head.

'Yes, yes, 'tis a painful thing,' said Mr *Shandy*, shaking his head too, but for reasons of his own rather than those of his brother.

During the earlier waiting, and before the arrival of Doctor *Slop*, a sudden increase in the sounds of activity above caused Mr *Shandy* to ask: 'What can they be doing, brother?'

'I think it would not be amiss, brother,' said the Captain, taking his pipe from his mouth and striking the ashes from it, 'if we rung the bell.'

In came *Obadiah* at the sound of the bell.

'Pray what's all that racket over our heads, *Obadiah*?' said Mr *Shandy*. 'My brother and I can scarce hear ourselves speak.'

'My Mistress is taken very badly,' said *Obadiah*.

'And why is *Susannah* running down the garden as if they were going to ravish her?'

'She is taking the shortest cut into town to fetch the old midwife.'

'Then saddle a horse and go directly for Dr *Slop* the man-midwife—and let him know your Mistress has fallen into labour. And that I desire he will return with you with all speed.'

'It is very strange,' said Mr *Shandy*, as *Obadiah* left, 'there being so expert an operator as Dr *Slop* nearby, that my wife should persist to the very last in this obstinate humour of hers, in trusting the life of my child—and not only the life of my child—but her own life, and with it the lives of all the children I might have begot out of her, to an uneducated crone.'

'Mayhap, brother, she does it to save the expense.'

'A pudding's end. The Doctor must be paid the same for inaction as action. If not better—to keep him in good temper.'

'Then it can only be out of modesty,' said the Captain. 'I dare say my sister-in-law does not care to let a man come so near… so near her… her backside,' said the blushing and bashful man.

'By heaven, brother *Toby*, you would try the patience of a *Job*.'

'On what account?'

'To think of a man living to your age, and knowing so little of women.'

'I know nothing at all about them, and my total ignorance of the sex gives me just cause to say that I neither know nor do pretend to know anything about them or their concerns.'

'Methinks, brother, you might at least know so much as the right end of a woman from the wrong.'

I observed, as often before, the differing, yet mutually affectionate brothers. Mr *Shandy* demonstrative and forceful in the expression of his opinions, the Captain responding mildly, untroubled by his brother's criticisms, frequently answering his brother's lengthy scientific and philosophical pronouncements with a single sentence of simple common sense. Any further discussion of the Captain's deficient knowledge of womanhood was prevented by the sudden, arrival of Dr *Slop* in a manner not of his choosing, nor befitting a man of his profession. His squat, uncourtly figure appeared in the parlour doorway splattered in mud, his hinder parts totally besmear'd, with little of the rest of him free from muddy stains and blotches. Leading the Doctor by the hand was *Obadiah*.

Chapter Two

Washed and rubbed down, Dr *Slop* now lay back in his chair warmed by the fire, and with a large glass of sherry in his hand. We had heard from *Obadiah* that, riding a coach horse, he had quickly covered the eight miles to the Doctor's house to find that Dr *Slop* was not there, so riding with equal speed he set off back to *Shandy Hall*. Not sixty yards from the *Hall*, round a sharp corner the speeding coach horse had collided with Dr *Slop* on his diminutive pony. Doctor and pony bowled over onto the road into the thick winter mud, as the heavy horse hurtled by. Being so close to the *Hall*, *Obadiah* did not attempt to remount the Doctor, but took him by the hand to the *Hall*.

Comfortable in his chair, the Doctor explained his presence on the road where the unhappy encounter with *Obadiah* occurred. He had been in the vicinity earlier to see a patient, and aware of Mrs *Shandy* coming near to her time, had been on his way to *Shandy Hall* to check on her condition. 'In spite of my mishap it is fortuitous that I am here,' he said, and struggled to rise from the chair against the weight of his stomach. Once on his feet Dr *Slop* made for the door until halted by Mr *Shandy* informing him that Mrs *Shandy* had requested the midwife, who was now attending the birth. The Doctor stopped in his tracks, turned, and sank back into his chair.

'Did you have the latest obstetric devices with you?' enquired Mr *Shandy*,

The Doctor sighed, 'I was not carrying my equipment with me.'

'We must have them to hand,' said Mr *Shandy*, and sent *Obadiah* to the Doctor's house again, promising him a crown if he made haste.

'The peculiar manner of your arrival,' said the Captain, addressing Dr *Slop*, 'instantly brought the great *Stevinus* into my head, who is a favourite author with me.'

'I will lay twenty guineas to a single crown piece,' interrupted his brother, 'that this *Stevinus* is directly or indirectly connected with the science of fortification.'

'He is so,' said the Captain.

'I knew it—though for the soul of me I cannot see what kind of connection there can be betwixt Dr *Slop's* sudden coming, and a discourse on fortification—yet I feared it. Talk of what we will brother, or let the occasion be never so foreign or unfit for the subject, you are bound to bring it in.'

Mr *Shandy* was in the habit of mocking his brother over this obsession with fortifications, calling it his 'hobby-horse'. Yet it was the hobby-horse that had enabled the Captain to ride to recovery from the disabling wound he received at the *Siege of Namur*, and his brother's scoffing made not the slightest dent in his deep enthusiasm for the subject. The Captain's fascination with fortifications came from that wounding. In the assault on the fortified city he was struck down by what was first thought to be a cannon ball, but proved to be a chunk of masonry broken off from the battlements by cannon fire. The severity of the wound due to the weight of the stone rather than to its projectile force.

'If I survive, *Trim*,' he said, lying in the hospital, his face riven with pain, 'you will still have a place with me.'

If the wound had proved fatal I cannot imagine how my life would have been.

Chapter Three

When the Captain was well enough to travel, his brother had him brought back to this country. Mr *Shandy* had established a trading company in *London*, and wishing to do all he could to help his stricken brother, assigned to him the best apartment in the *London* house. For four years the Captain, whom I continued to serve, remained there, he initially confined to his bed and then to his room.

To help keep up the Captain's spirits any visitor or acquaintance of Mr *Shandy* who came to the house, would be taken by the hand and led upstairs to see his damaged brother, where they would chat by the bedside for an hour or so. Naturally curious about the wound, and generally of a belief that the telling of a soldier's wound beguiles the pain of it, the visitors would ask the Captain about it. He found difficulty in answering their questions, being too shy in his modesty to describe the wound to his groin—the surgeon and I the only ones to know the exact nature of the injuries—so he focussed on the circumstances in which it was received.

'At *Namur* I was taking part in the memorable *English* and *Dutch* attack on the gate of *St Nicholas*,' he would tell his visitors. 'We were at the point of the advanced counterscarp before the gate, and terribly exposed to the shot of the counter-guard and demi-bastion of *St Roch*. My wound was got in one of the traverses, about thirty toises from the returning angle of the trench opposite to the salient angle of the demi-bastion of *St Roch*.'

'Toises?' visitors would ask.

'It is customary to use this French measurement when discussing fortifications,' he explained. 'A toise is about six English feet.'

His account of the situation at *Namur* was often difficult to comprehend even to the military men who called on him. His attempts to describe the complexity of continental fortifications, the counterscarps, ravelins, curtins, glacis, and gasons, among which the action had taken place, proved difficult and frustrating for the Captain. And acting out of kindness for his brother, Mr *Shandy* was continually introducing fresh friends and fresh inquirers. In an effort to give his account of the harrowing event more clarity, he collected books on military architecture and the science of fortifications. These he studied during the many hours of his immobilisation within his brother's home. Though it was only when he acquired a large map of the fortifications of the town and citadel of *Namur*, which I pasted upon a board, that he was freed from sad explanations, and able to stick a pin upon the identical spot where he had been struck down. His increasing knowledge and understanding gave him confidence to extend his accounts to encompass the broader aspects of the siege.

The Captain's desire to repeatedly relive the event of his wounding seemed to be a way of coming to terms with the cruel blow he had received. The chunk of stone had been dislodged by our own canon fire. His interest in the science of military fortifications grew, becoming an endeavour in itself, and with it a rising of his spirits from the despondency that had taken hold of him. Immersed in his books he ranged beyond *Namur* and obtained plans and histories of sieges throughout *Flanders* and *Italy*. He became impatient with his confinement and lengthy treatment, anxious for his wound to be healed, and it seemed that the wound responded. 'It is beginning to incarnate, and if there is no further exfoliation,' the surgeon informed him, 'it would likely be dried up within a few weeks.'

The Captain was finding the table on which he laid out his maps and plans, to be no longer adequate for their proper representation, and he asked me to measure it and get one twice the size. 'I think,' I said, pointing to a map of *Dunkirk* pinned on the wall, 'that these ravelins, bastions, curtins, and horn works, make but a poor work of it here upon paper. You will soon be well enough to go down to the country,' I told him. 'Where on a rood or rood and a half of ground, I could throw up the earth to make models of these paper plans.'

His eyes brightened immediately, and colour came into his face. I could see he was filled with joy by my idea. 'My house near *Shandy Hall*,' he murmured, and slept little that night. In the morning, without delay, he hired a carriage and four into which I packed, along with the books and maps, a pioneer's spade and a bundle of lint and dressings. Telling no one, afraid his brother would try to dissuade him, and leaning heavily on my shoulder, the Captain, with the help of his crutch, took his first steps outside the house in four years. As soon as he was safely installed in the carriage we left for the village where the *Shandy* estate lay, to his neat little country house which had, beyond the kitchen garden, a bowling-green of about two roods.

Within days of our arrival I began digging up the bowling-green turf to construct a model of the fortifications at *Namur*. The Captain, leaning on his crutch, and holding the plans showing the type of fortification and disposition, and I exchanging my stick for a spade. Glad to be in the open air, and as eager as the Captain on transforming the flat paper drawings into the bulk of solid earth. This became our regular occupation, our activities obscured from the curious eyes of villagers by holly bushes and a thick yew hedge.

One local resident with particular interest in the arrival of the Captain, was widow *Wadman*, whose house and garden ran alongside. With great willingness she had provided accommodation those first few days whilst the Captain's house was fitted out with furniture and beds. There I first made the acquaintance of *Bridget*, her lively, dark-haired attendant.

Mr *Shandy* had not been pleased by his brother's sudden and unannounced departure, and disapproving of the Captain's intentions in moving to the village house. But by the time of *Tristram's* birth it had been our home for nearly twenty years. Over this period almost every square inch of the bowling-green had been excavated and shaped to represent the fortifications existing at sieges and battles which had taken place across *Europe*. During this time Mr *Shandy* had ceased his trading activities in *London* and returned to *Shandy Hall*. The Captain told me that his brother had developed firm views about the situation in *London*. He says that the flow of men and money towards the metropolis has set in so strong, as to become dangerous to our civil rights. His answer would be to send back to their legal settlements, all who had only frivolous reasons for descending on *London*, thereby ensuring that the metropolis would not totter through its own weight, and the rest of the country would be restored to its due share of nourishment and flourish once more. 'We are well fitted here, *Trim*, into these my brother's notions,' the Captain said.

4

Alan, who rarely read more than a newspaper, made slow progress with the manuscript, finding difficulty in understanding the strange English it was written in. He persevered, making an effort each night to get through a few more of the faded pages, driven by a conviction that within them he would find evidence of their value. The cottage too, as the place of discovery, likely to be worth more by having a literary association. His progress quickened as he became more familiar with the language of James Butler. He began to look forward to his nightly reading, and entering into the world of Corporal Trim. The time he spent with the pages increased.

'I can't get a word out of you once you pick up those papers,' Wendy complained. 'What do you find in that old stuff?'

'It's about a book written by a man called Tristram Shandy, telling of his family who lived somewhere near the cottage in the old days. Wealthy people living in a hall with lots of servants.'

'How long ago?'

'You know history—when was there a King William who came from Holland?'

'William of Orange?'

'That'll be him—the Dutch national strip is orange.'

'It must be about four hundred years ago. I could make some enquiries at the library about these papers.'

'We'll keep this to ourselves until we're ready. I don't want other people muscling-in on it.'

The next evening when Alan picked up the bundle he saw that it was tied differently from the way he had left it.

Chapter Four

Dr *Slop's* maid gave *Obadiah* the green bays bag with the Doctor's instruments in it, exhorting him to put his head and one arm through the strings, and ride with it slung across his body. So saying she undid the bow-knot to lengthen the strings, and helped him on with it. To prevent the instruments flying out in galloping back at the speed *Obadiah* intended, he pursed up the open mouth of the bag with half a dozen hard knots, each of which he had twitched and drawn together with all the strength of his body. Eager to merit the promised crown, he galloped off, accompanied by the music of jangling obstetrical instruments. He delivered the green bag and received his crown.

A sudden trampling overhead caused Dr *Slop* to pick up the green bag and attempted to untie the knots. 'By all that's unfortunate,' he muttered, 'the thing will actually befall me as it is.' And he cursed *Obadiah* for his knots. 'Pox take the fellow, I shall never get these knots untied as long as I live. Lend me a penknife—I must e'en cut the knots at last.' Blood appeared on the Doctor's hand, and he issued a stream of curses against poor *Obadiah*. 'My thumb is cut quite across to the very bone—I am undone for this bout. The man should be shot.'

'Small curses, Dr *Slop*,' said Mr *Shandy*, who had great respect for *Obadiah*, 'are but waste of our strength and soul's health to no manner of purpose.'

'I own it,' said the Doctor.

'They are like sparrow shot,' the Captain said.

'They serve,' continued Mr *Shandy*, 'to stir the humours—but carry off none of their acrimony. For my own part, I seldom swear or curse at all. But if I fall into it by surprise, I try to hold to my belief that a wise and just man would always endeavour to proportion the vent given to these humours. I have the greatest veneration for the gentleman, who, in distrust of his own discretion in this point, sat down and composed fit forms of swearing for all occasions. He kept them ever by him, on the chimney piece within his reach, ready for use.'

'I never apprehended,' said Dr *Slop*, 'that such a thing was ever thought of.'

'I was reading one of them to my brother this morning—but 'tis too violent for a cut of the thumb.'

'The impediment of my cut thumb,' said the Doctor, 'will be overcome by my new forceps, which subordinates the use of fingers and thumbs.' And he produced the instrument from the green bag. 'I will show you,' he said, grasping the Captain's hands.

'Upon my honour, sir,' the Captain cried out, 'you have tore every bit of the skin quite off the back of both my hands with your forceps, and have crushed all my knuckles to a jelly into the bargain.'

''Tis your own fault,' said Dr *Slop*, 'you should have clinch'd your two fists together in the form of a child's head, as I told you.'

'I did so,' answered the Captain.

'Then the points of my forceps have not been sufficiently arm'd, or the rivet wants closing—or else the cut on my thumb has made me little awkward,' said the Doctor.

''Tis well,' said Mr *Shandy*, 'that the experiment was not first made on my child's head.'

'It would not have been a cherry stone the worse—a child's head is as soft as the pap of an apple.'

Consideration of the use of this latest design in birthing instruments was interrupted by *Susannah* rushing in looking flustered: 'My poor mistress is ready to faint—and the drops are done—and the bottle of julap is broke. The child is still where it was—the nurse has cut her arm—and the midwife has fallen backwards on the edge of the fender, her hip bruised as black as your hat.'

'I'll look at it,' said Dr *Slop*.

'Better you look at my mistress,' said *Susannah*. 'The midwife desires you go up this moment where she will gladly give you an account of how things are.'

'It would be proper if the midwife came down to me,' said Dr *Slop*. He wrapped a handkerchief around his bleeding thumb, collected his green bag and, for a man of his size, tripped nimbly across the room to follow *Susannah* up the stairs.

I left the Captain and his brother still conversing about the nature of curses, and went in search of a pair of old jackboots with an idea of turning them into mortars for a battle scene. A suitable pair found, I took them across to the house. When I returned to the *Hall* both brothers were asleep. The sound of the creaking door hinge woke Mr *Shandy*.

'All is quiet and hush, at least above stairs—I hear not one foot stirring. Prithee *Trim*, what is the noise in the kitchen?'

'It is Dr *Slop* making a bridge,' I told him.

'A bridge—a drawbridge?' the Captain now awake, alerted by this suggestion of a fortification.

'For the baby, the boy's nose was damaged in the delivery,' I said. '*Susannah* says it's as flat as a pancake. The Doctor is making a false bridge with a piece of cotton and a thin piece of whalebone out of *Susannah's* stays.'

'The Doctor crushed my knuckles with his fancy forceps,' said the Captain.

Mr *Shandy*, from a family proud of their distinctive noses, became distressed by news of this injury to his son, and, attended by his brother, took to his room. There, I learned, he threw himself prostrate on the bed, and lay stretched across it as still as if the hand of death had pushed him down. It was a good hour and a half before the Captain had the relief of seeing some movement from his brother. First from the foot which hung over the bedside, and in a few moments from the hand, the knuckles of which had all the time reclined on the handle of the chamber-pot. 'Did ever man,' he said, raising himself and turning to face his brother, who was sitting with his chin resting on his crutch. 'Did ever a poor unfortunate man, brother *Toby*, receive so many lashes?'

'His speaking of lashes,' the Captain told me later, 'had me thinking of the poor grenadier in *Makay's* regiment.'

'Oh God! *Dick Johnson*, and he was innocent,' cried I, 'and he whipped almost to death's door. They had better have shot him outright, as he begg'd, and he gone directly to heaven. His soul scourged out of his body for the ducats another man put in his knapsack.'

Mr *Shandy* was driven by a conviction that fine noses in a family were a mark of its distinction, this tenet in favour of long noses taking root in the *Shandy* family over several generations. It seems the issue had surfaced in connection with the great grandparents' marriage settlement. When the great grandfather had objected to a proposed jointure of £300, considering it to be an unreasonable amount for a bride who had only £2,000, her justification was; 'it is because you have little or no nose, Sir.' Now that he had a son whose nose had suffered a shortening at birth, *Walter Shandy* set about the accommodation of this unwelcome fact within his philosophical landscape. He began by collecting every book and treatise which had been systematically wrote upon noses, though these were not many.

One story on noses I heard directly from Mr *Shandy*, who recounted *Hafen Slawkenbergius's Tale* in spoken English to his brother and I, conscious that the Captain's Latin was deficient, and knowing I had none. It was the story of *Diego*, a man with an extremely large nose, travelling by mule through *Strasburg*, on his way to *Frankfurt*. His enormous nose incites attention, some alleging it to be false, and others, usually the women, believing it to be real and intent upon touching it. The tale drags on, enlivened only by *Walter Shandy's* enthusiastic telling. I could see from the way the Captain became pre-occupied with his pipe, that he too was losing interest in *Hafen Slawkenbergius*. The pipe oft taken from his mouth, its length seriously contemplated as he held it between finger and thumb, surveying it transversely, then this way and that, in all possible directions and foreshortenings. His brother, engrossed in this story of noses, continued unaware that he was not carrying his two listeners with him.

I don't know what effect Mr *Shandy's* readings about noses had upon his attitude to noses, but he had already resolved to give the child a prestigious name to compensate for the lack of a commanding nose. 'He shall be christened *Trismegistus*,' he told the Captain, 'the thrice-wise *Greek* god.'

'My brother has a strong belief that names influence the character of the bearer,' the Captain told me, 'and he has a particular aversion to the name *Tristram*. He says who has ever heard tell of a man called *Tristram*, perform any thing great or worth recording. My brother had no hand in naming the other son, *Robert*, in his opinion a name of neutral influence, as he happened to be at Epsom when the name was given.'

On the day of the christening Mr *Shandy* was roused unexpectedly by *Susannah*. 'There's not a moment to lose—the child is black in the face and in a fit. The curate's in the dressing room with the child upon his knee—waiting for a name. My mistress bid me run as fast as I could to get the name.'

'I'll get up and dressed.'

'There is no time for that—the child's as black as my shoe.'

'*Trismegistus*. Can you remember, *Trismegistus*?'

She ran with all speed along the gallery, repeating the unfamiliar name.

''Tis Tris… Tris—' she said to the curate.

'*Tristram*, which is my name,' he said.

'Then 'tis *Tristramgistus*,' said *Susannah*.

'There is no *gistus*,' the curate said, dipping his hand into the water.

Mr *Shandy* arrived at the half-open door, a night gown on his arm, and one hand holding up his breeches.

'She has not forgot the name?' he asked.

'No, no,' the curate assured him, and he returned along the gallery and to bed.

To the Captain later that morning, he said; 'If my wife will but venture him—brother *Toby*, *Trismegistus* shall be dressed and brought down to us, whilst you and I are getting our breakfast together.—*Obadiah*, go tell *Susannah* to step here.'

'She is run up stairs this very instant,' said *Obadiah*, 'sobbing and crying, and wringing her hands as if her heart would break.'

'We shall have a rare month of it, brother *Toby*.'

''Tis some misfortune,' the Captain told him.

'That it is, to have so many elements breaking loose, and riding in triumph in every corner of a gentleman's house. What's the matter *Susannah*?' Who stood red-eyed at the door.

'They have called the child *Tristram*—and my mistress is just got out of an hysterical fit about it. 'Tis not my fault—I told him it was *Tristram-gistus*.'

'Make tea for yourself, brother *Toby*,' said *Walter Shandy* softly, and took down his hat with the gentlest movement of limbs, that ever affliction harmonised and attuned together, and walked out to the fish pond.

At this time on that day my concern was with a different event. A cow had broken into the garden and its presence had caused some damage to the model fortifications. I went to the *Hall* to tell the Captain and found him in the parlour.

'You have heard, I imagine, of this unlucky accident—'

'O yes, *Trim*,' he said.

'It was not in the least owing to me,' I said, which brought a puzzled look to his face.

34

'To thee? It was *Susannah's* and the curate's folly between them.' And he told me of the child's christening. I then informed him of the cow among the fortifications, both of us smiling at our misunderstanding.

This scene is completely recast in *Tristram Shandy's* account, implying that I took advantage of the misfortune of the christening to avoid mention of the cow's incursion or suggestion of blame. His version has *Trim* thinking; *the mischief the cow has done in breaking into the fortifications may be told his honour hereafter,* and writes, *Trim's casuistry and his address, under the cover of his low bow, prevented all suspicion in my uncle Toby.'*

The Captain and I discussed the importance of a name and the possible influence it could have on the subsequent character of the person who bore it.

'For my part, *Trim*, I can see little or no difference betwixt my nephew being called *Tristram* or *Trismegistus*,' he said. 'Yet as the thing sits so near my brother's heart, I would freely have given a hundred pounds rather than it should have happened,'

'A hundred pounds,' I said, 'I would not give a cherry stone.'

'Nor would I, *Trim*, on my own account—but my brother, whom there is no arguing with in this case—maintains that a great deal more depends upon Christian names than what ignorant people imagine. He insists that there never was a great or heroic action performed since the world began by one called *Tristram*—nay he will have it, *Trim*, that a *Tristram* can neither be learned, or wise, or brave.'

"'Tis all a fancy,' I said, 'for I fought just as well when the regiment called me *Trim*, as when they called me *James Butler*.'

'And for my own part,' the Captain said, 'though I should blush to boast of myself—had my name been *Alexander*, I could have done no more at *Namur* than my duty.'

'Bless you,' I said, 'does a man think of his Christian name when he goes on the attack?'

'Or when he stands in the trench?' said the Captain.

'Or when he enters a breech?'

'Or forces the lines?'

'Or facing a platoon?'

'Or when he marches up the glacis,' concluded the Captain.

Our military reminiscences ended when Mr *Shandy* returned from the fish pond, hung up his hat, sat down, and began this lamentation.

It is in vain longer, to struggle as I have done against this most uncomfortable of human persuasions—I see it plainly that either for my own sins, brother Toby, or the sins and follies of the Shandy family, heaven has thought fit to draw forth the heaviest of its artillery against me; and that the prosperity of my child is the point upon which the whole force of it is directed to play... Whether calmness and serenity of mind in your sister, with a due attention, brother Toby, to her evacuations and repletions—and the rest of her non-naturals, might not, in the course of nine months gestation, have set all things to rights,—My child was bereft of these!—What a teazing life did she lead herself, and consequently her foetus too, with that nonsensical anxiety about lying in the town? What battles did she fight with me, and what perpetual storms about the midwife.

It was when he criticised Mrs *Shandy's* attitude that the Captain was driven to come to her defence. 'I thought my sister submitted with the greatest patience,' he said. 'I never heard her utter one fretful word about it. We will send for Mr *Yorick.*'

'You may send for whom you will.'

We were joined by parson *Yorick,* who avoided being drawn into a family argument by telling a story about the King of France and names.

'It would not be amiss, *Francis* the First of *France* said to his first minister, if this good understanding betwixt ourselves and *Switzerland* was a little strengthened. There is no end, Sire, replied the minister, in giving money to these people—they would swallow up the treasury of *France*. There are more ways of bribing states besides that of giving money, said the king, I'll pay *Switzerland* the honour of standing godfather for my next child. In so doing, your majesty, you would have all the grammarians in *Europe* upon your back, *Switzerland*, as a republic being female, can in no construction be godfather. Then she may be godmother, said the king.

They take it kindly, the minister informed the king, but the republic as godmother claims her right in naming the child. In all reason she will christen him *Francis*, or *Henry*, or *Lewes*, or some name she knows will be agreeable to us. You are deceived, the name the republic has chosen is *Shadrach*. By saint *Peter's* girdle, cried the king, I'll have nothing to do with the *Swiss*. We are too much involved with them, the minister told him. We'll pay them in money, said the king. Sire, there are not sixty thousand crowns in the treasury. I'll pawn the best jewels in my crown—they are already pawned, said the minister. Then by heavens we'll go to war with 'em, the king said.'

Chapter Five

The misnamed child survived to produce his misnamed and misleading book. Within it the opinions expressed are to a great extent those of the father, *Walter Shandy*, and the description of me a travesty of the truth. Corporal *Trim* is portrayed as a servile servant, forever bowing and scraping, and constantly addressing his master, *'your Honour'* and always prefacing a wish to speak with an *'if it please your Honour'* when in reality the Captain and I spoke to one another without such formality. *Tristram*, who admired *Cervantes* beyond all other authors, has been greatly influenced by *Don Quixote*. It is as though he wishes to cast me in the mould of *Sancho Panza* and the Captain as a *Don Quixote* figure. One of the benefits of spending the four years in *London* with the Captain, was use of the extensive library in his brother's house, and which included the most recent translation of *Don Quixote*. By the time we left I had read it and nearly everything else in the library apart from books in Latin or Greek. Yet the corporal is presented as uneducated whose ability even to read is remarkable, as if he were a dog who had learned to walk upright on its hind legs.

I can understand why *Tristram* forbears to mention the time when I accompanied the family on a tour of *Europe*, and of when in the *Netherlands* I was the only one with sufficient of the Dutch language to negotiate our requirements. The Latin, Greek, or even French, spoken by those assuming the superiority of their education, proving of little use. My Dutch learned in the ranks of the army during the campaigns with our Dutch allies.

There is little recognition by *Tristram* of the crucial part I played in the Captain's recovery, who, without my encouragement, I believe would have remained an invalid confined to his room. It is my consolation that the Captain knew this to be true, and his appreciation of my role in his recuperation the foundation of our friendship. A friendship which is the reason why, against opposition from *Tristram* and the *Shandy* family, I am living in the Captain's former house and have money enough to produce this book. 'In recompence, *Trim*,' the Captain said, 'of thy long fidelity to me, and that goodness of thy heart I have had such proof of.'

In writing this book I am describing events as they really were, and not as they are presented by *Tristram Shandy* as if he were a later *Cervantes* engaged in manufacturing a new *Don Quixote* and *Sancho Panza*. I also seek to bring attention to the manner of writing employed by *Tristram*, which is of such strangeness and peculiarity that questions his ability to give any believable account.

So what of my life before I appeared in *Tristram's* book?

Chapter Six

My father died of a fever when I was quite young and it was Grandfather *Naylor*, living with us, who had a great influence on my life. We were a Baptist family living in *Colchester* where my father, a master carpenter, had established a successful business, often responsible for building whole houses, as he had with the one in which we lived. Although not poor, my brother and I were unable to go to university, attendance barred to Dissenters, as all followers of non-approved religions were labelled. My education came from members of the Baptist community; it was thorough in all but the Latin and Greek languages. Reflecting the Baptist's view that church services should be conducted only in the language of the people. I revered my grandfather and spent many hours listening to him telling of his experiences as a cavalry trooper in *Cromwell's* New Model Army. I would see him on his horse in his buff leather coat, wearing a lobster-tailed pot helmet, galloping forward, the reins in the gauntlet of his left hand, a sword in his right hand, a pistol in the saddle holster. He said the Royalists often fought bravely but lacked discipline, some of their officers too intent on personal glory. He told how they were routed at *Naseby*.

Much as I relished his descriptions of cavalry charges and the excitement of battle, it was his memory of the debates at *Putney* which left me with a more lasting impression. 'In the church there,' he said. '1647—we thought the world was about to change.' He told me of ordinary soldiers arguing with their Generals for greater democracy. Demanding a new constitution which would ensure the rights of the common people, ending oppressive laws, and allow freedom of worship. All men given the right to vote. My grandfather said it was all set out in *The Agreement of the People,* a document drawn up by *John Lilburne* and other Agitators in the New

Model Army. One of the men putting forward the proposals was identified only as '*Bedfordshire Man.*' 'But I knew him,' my grandfather said, 'he was Trooper *Weale* who I had served with in Colonel *Whalley's Regiment.*'

'It was a time when anything seemed possible,' my grandfather said. 'Even the air we breathed felt different. *New Jerusalem* was here—or so we thought.' He would give a deep sigh, and gaze silently into the flickering embers of the fire. The longing for the return of such a miraculous time has remained with me.

My mother's memories, a girl during the Civil War, were different from those of the former trooper, and ones I'd given little heed to until, in *Ireland* and in *Flanders*, I saw the suffering that war brought on a country's people. Vivid in her memory was the siege of *Colchester*, when the Royalists occupied the town and were besieged by the Parliamentarians. The water supply was cut off and food soon ran out. 'At first we ate horsemeat, then it was dog,' my mother said. 'We were starving, and when the siege ended after nearly three months there was not a cat left alive in the town.'

Chapter Seven

When Grandfather *Naylor* died I straightway enlisted in King *William's* army, my head full of grandfather's exploits as a soldier. My first experience of battle was in *Ireland* at the *River Boyne*, serving in Captain *Shandy's* company in a Regiment of Foot. Apart from their artillery fire we had no direct contact with the enemy, King *William* preferring to use his more experienced Dutch and German troops in the main action across the river. King *James* fled back to *France* and we besieged *Limerick* where the French and Irish troops had taken refuge. In the regiment I had become known as *Trim*, probably because of my ability to neatly pen orders and suchlike, which I was regularly called upon to do, my education superior to that of the average soldier. The other consequence of a sound education was that I was made corporal and taken on as Captain *Shandy's* personal man. But King *William's* army was not the New Model Army and there was little prospect of ever becoming an officer, especially for a Dissenter.

The siege at *Limerick* became prolonged, even the best Dutch troops unable to overcome the strong resistance put up by the garrison. Our regiment was encamped in the surrounding boggy countryside where almost every day there was rain. Disease spread through the camp and men began to die. The Captain and I both fell ill with the flux, and by the time the siege was raised were scarce able to crawl out of our tent. The Captain believed it was the Dutch juniper drink, geneva, which was the reason for our survival. Brandy too played a part, not to drink but for me to burn a dish of it each night to dry out the air inside his tent. I was truly relieved when we left *Ireland* and went with King *William's* army to *Flanders*.

From my army pay I sent money to my mother whose circumstances were much reduced since my brother *Tom* left home. He'd not had much success in his attempt to revive our father's business and had left the country to seek his fortune elsewhere. It was much later that we learned he had fetched up in *Lisbon* and had become married to a widow who had a sausage-making business.

He sent an account of the wedding and of the events that had led to his marriage, and I could see *Tom* in his white dimity and breeches passing jollily along the *Lisbon* street, swinging his stick, with a smile and a cheerful word for everyone. When he heard that the Jewish sausage maker had died and his widow was carrying on the business alone, he decided to offer his services. So without any introduction to the widow, except that of buying a pound of sausages, and as she prepared these began his courtship by a discourse on sausages, how they were made, with what meats, herbs and spices. What he had to say on the subject of sausages was kindly taken, and he went on to help her a little in the making of them.

In his letter *Tom* speaks of the negro girl he found in the sausage shop, flapping away flies with a bunch of white feathers tied to the end of a long cane. The poor friendless girl had suffered much persecution, and it was she who later led to a discussion with the Captain as to whether a Negro had a soul.

'I am not much versed in things of that kind,' he said, 'but I suppose God would not leave him without one, any more than thee or me.'

'It would be putting one sadly over the head of another,' I said.

'It would so,' he said.

'Why then is a black wench to be used worse than a white one?'

'I can give no reason,' said the Captain.

'It is because she has no one to stand up for her.'

'"Tis that very thing, *Trim,* which recommends her to protection—and her brethren with her. 'Tis the fortune of war which has put the whip into our hands now—where it will be hereafter, heaven knows!—but be it where it will, the brave, *Trim,* should not use it unkindly.'

'God forbid,' I said.

Tom's letter came with some presents, among them a scarlet Montero cap of finest Spanish cloth and mounted all round with fur. A light blue embroidered piece at the front showed that it had been the property of a Portuguese cavalryman. I treasure the Montero cap to this day, wearing it on special occasions. Later came the dreadful news that *Tom* had been taken by the Inquisition—taken in the middle of the night out of his bed where he was lying with his wife, seemingly for having married a Jew. It grieved me terribly to think of my brother's misfortune and of my helplessness in the face of his sufferings.

My own suffering began at the *Battle of Landen.* We were in *Flanders* deployed by King *William* to help in opposing the French expansion into *Europe.* The British army had been increased and was being equipped with improved weapons. In our regiment the old matchlock muskets had been replaced by the new flintlocks. These were easier to use, making it possible to get off as many as three shots within a minute. And no longer having to avoid the danger of a lighted match igniting a neighbour's powder box, we were able to stand almost shoulder to shoulder when we faced the enemy. With the flintlock came the socket bayonet, reducing the need for pikemen in the file, our bayonets now the defence against cavalry.

The worst time in battle came even before the first shot was fired, standing silently in line, facing an enemy close enough to make out details of their uniforms. Awaiting the order to fire, expecting at any moment to receive a volley from the opposing ranks. At those times I would willingly have put myself in my grandfather's place, galloping forward on his horse, sword in hand. Once the firing had started, the disciplined task of reloading and maintaining a rate of fire took over our thoughts, though often we followed our first volley with a bayonet charge. In the hand to hand fighting most of the wounds were from bayonets. Such was the case at *Landen* where, outnumbered by the French, we fought hard to repel their repeated assaults on our lines.

But it was a musket ball that disabled me, taken in the knee and leaving me lying helpless on the ground. Shortly afterwards the French cavalry broke through and rode over us, our army routed. In the rapid retreat I, and the other wounded, were left where we had fallen. The noise of battle moved away, leaving an oppressive silence broken only by cries of the wounded. Unable to move, I lay there in great pain and growing thirst, around me the bodies of my comrades. In periods of lucidity I saw dark figures of women moving over the battlefield, but these were no angels of mercy bringing me the water my body craved, their business was scavenging the dead for anything of value. When night came on I was fearful of marauders. It was not until noon the next day that we were exchanged and I was put in a cart with a dozen others to be taken to our hospital.

The severe pain I had endured as I lay on the ground became unbearable in the jolting cart, with the loss of blood and the onset of a fever it was more than I could sustain. At a peasants' house where we stopped I was taken in and a young woman gave me a drink of a cordial, and further drinks when she saw how welcome they were to me. I told her of the intolerable anguish I was in as she helped me back to the cart, and said that I would much rather lie down on a bed and die than go back on it. When I fainted away in her arms she persuaded them to go on without me, saying that I would expire immediately if I were put on the cart.

When I came to myself I found I was lying on a bed in a still and quiet cottage with no one but the young woman, and the peasant and his wife. The woman was beside me holding to my nose a corner of her handkerchief dipped in vinegar, and rubbing my temple with her other hand. At first I took her to be the peasants' daughter but when I offered her a little purse of florins, she called the old man and his wife and showed them the money to assure them they would receive payment for my accommodation. This, and her manner of speaking, as well as by her apparel, dressed down to her toes in black, with her hair concealed under a cambric border, told me she could not be their daughter. She had the appearance of a nun, and I later learned that there were such nuns in this part of Flanders who are not confined to the cloisters but visit and take care of the sick.

She became my nurse, soothing me through the fever and fomenting my knee until it began to heal. She was almost constantly at my bedside, and if she left the room my heart sickened, recovering only on her return. Her soothing hands were softer than satin, yet I resisted the desire she aroused in me. The nearest I came to breaking my resolve not to sully this angel was an occasion when I seized and kissed her hand. After three weeks I was in a condition to be moved to the hospital and never again saw the woman who was my first love.

In his book my account of this love is portrayed by *Tristram Shandy* in a crude manner, as if I had little sensibility and were a simpleton such as *Sancho Panza*. What was in truth a nursing procedure to bring movement back the leg, in the book he describes it in this manner: *The more she rubbed, and the longer strokes she took—the more the fire kindled in my veins—till at length, by two or three strokes longer than the rest—my passion rose to the highest pitch.* In this way is the story of the nun and I distorted into a lascivious tale of physical contact, the kind of prurience which would attract a certain type of reader. The impression given is that this is the only way love can be experienced by someone of the lower orders. Whereas it was the purity of that love, and my resistance to heated desire beyond kissing her hand, which I had recounted.

With my knee much healed the journey to the hospital caused me a deal less pain than I had suffered when carted off the battlefield. Yet I was in dire spirits, leaving a woman I had fallen in love with, and no longer suitable for the army. I faced a life of penury. It was Captain *Shandy* who saved me from a bleak future. He visited me at the hospital and ensured that I had sufficient provisions. He told me that, although with a lame leg I would not be fit for active service, he would employ me as his private servant. This was greatly to my liking, even though I would be carrying a walking-stick in place of a musket, for the Captain was a man I was used to working with and had grown to respect. He had none of the belligerence associated with martial and military men, yet he was well respected by his troops, gained by his cool bravery in battle and his fair dealings in the administration of the Company.

It took a while before I could use my left leg again, but as soon I was able get about with the aid of a stick I made my way to where the regiment were re-grouped. I was welcomed by the Captain and remained with him for the rest of his life, a life almost cut short at the *Siege of Namur*. Then began the years of the Captain's recuperation at his brother's house in *London*, living there until we came to this house which has since become mine.

5

Alan found Trim's account of his background easier to read and more understandable than the earlier section. He was gripped by the corporal's description of his army experiences, of him lying wounded and being carried off the battlefield on a cart. No anaesthetics in those days—Alan could almost feel the pain, but he literally winced at Captain Shandy's wound. He never knew history could be so interesting. The only thing he could remember from school was 1066 and the Battle of Hastings.

'What's the flux?' he asked Wendy.

'I'm not sure— I'll look it up.' Wendy was attached to her laptop, spending time with Facebook and suchlike things, which had no attraction for Alan.

'It's dysentery, blood and diarrhoea—ugh,' she said, a few minutes later.

'God! It must have been awful—hundreds of 'em stuck in tents,' he said. 'And imagine having to stand in line expecting to be shot at. They were brave—soldiers in those days.'

'Things haven't changed much. My grandfather would have been stood waiting to go over the top into the bullets at Paschendale.'

Chapter Eight

A strange aspect of *Tristram's* book is that he frequently falls into a manner of writing as if he was in direct conversation with a reader. He does this to deny that, in the section on his christening, he had given a wrong impression of his mother's religious leanings.

How could you, Madam, be so inattentive in reading the last chapter? I told you in it, 'That my mother was not a papist,—Papist! You told me no such thing, Sir. Madam, I beg leave to repeat it over again. That I told you, at least, as words, by direct inference, could tell you such a thing.—Then, Sir, I must have miss'd a page.—No, Madam, you have not miss'd a page.—Then I was asleep, Sir.—My pride, Madam, cannot allow you that refuge.—Then, I declare, I know nothing at all about the matter.—That, Madam, is the very fault I lay to your charge; and as a punishment for it, I do insist upon it, that you immediately turn back, that is, as soon as you get to the next full stop, and read the whole chapter over again.

This outburst had been prompted by his account of discussions about the possibility of nullifying his christening, and in which the different procedures and requirements of the Roman Catholic Church had been raised. The attempt to replace the name *Tristram* continued when his father was invited to a dinner given for a gathering of high-ranking church officials. He disliked *'these great dinners,'* but was persuaded by parson *Yorick* that it would be an opportunity to learn if there was any way the christening could be undone. He asked the Captain to attend the dinner with him. *Obadiah* and I, on two coach horses, led the cavalcade, the Captain in his laced regimental jacket and tye-wig rode alongside his brother. He told me that the intention had been to make the journey by coach, but his brother discovered that the family coat-of-arms it bore, was not changed from that at the time of his marriage. The incorporation of his wife's coat-of-arms to the *Shandy* family arms had resulted in what looked like a band sinister, and Mr *Shandy* refused to go to the dinner in a coach bearing this sign of illegitimacy. Parson *Yorick* told him that one of the things the clergy knew least about was heraldry, but Mr *Shandy* still insisted on riding to the dinner.

The dinner was not without incident, the Captain said later. Hot roasted chestnuts were brought to the table, and hands reached for them into the damask napkin in which they were wrapped. One of the chestnuts rolled off the table and dropped into the aperture of a churchman's breeches. He uttered an oath and leapt up, throwing the offending chestnut onto the floor. He was a man with whom parson *Yorick* had long been at odds, arising from *Yorick's* sharp criticism of a doctrinal treatise the churchman had written. He suspected *Yorick*, who was seated close by, of being the cause of the painful encounter with the chestnut. His suspicion became hardened when he saw the parson pick up the offending chestnut and, considering it no worse for its adventure, proceed to eat it.

The incident instigated a discussion among these church dignitaries, as to the best treatment for easing the burning pain caused by the heated chestnut. One made the suggestion that the tender part should be wrapped in the soft paper just come off a printer's press. It is the oil and lamp black with which such paper is impregnated that does the business, said another. If that is so, someone said, then spread them thickly on a rag, and clap it on directly. The offended man looked on, his face rigid, his eyes glaring with hate at *Yorick*.

There followed consideration by the scholarly men present, of the matter that was foremost in Mr *Shandy's* mind; the possibility of a re-christening for his son. He enjoyed and appreciated the subtleties of their learned discourses, though the conclusion they arrived at finally ended any hope of giving *Tristram* some other name.

6

Curiosity drove Wendy to see what Alan was reading in the old papers. Unwilling to admit her interest in this find from the cottage, she read them when she was alone in the flat, carefully replacing the package before she expected Alan to be back. *The Corporal's Story* was unlike anything Wendy had read before, usually popular novels she got from the library, and it took an effort to get into. What urged her on were the feelings aroused by the descriptions of Tristram's birth. Although horrified by what the mother had to endure to have the child, she was envious of the fertile Mrs Shandy, and would willingly have faced similar suffering in her desperation for a baby. Reading of the events at Shandy Hall brought up painful memories of the years of false hopes and disappointment. Always when she thinks of those times, it is her mother who looms large in her mind. From the time of Wendy's marriage her mother's eagerness to become a grandmother dominated their relationship. In the early days, when there was still hope of becoming pregnant, she put up with her mother's insistent questioning. But as time passed, and her mother began to lose hope of a grandchild, she acted as though it was her daughter's fault, intensifying Wendy's own feelings of being deficient; of being barren. For her own sanity Wendy broke off all contact with her mother.

She missed seeing her dad and used to arrange to meet him on his rounds in York where he worked as a postman. This ended when he retired and her parents moved to Bridlington. They had been living in Bridlington for almost two years when she visited them. Feeling stronger since living with Alan, and able to face her mother for the chance to see her dad again. Her mother's reception was cool, but her father was delighted to see his daughter. It was clear from what he told her that it was his wife who had wanted to move to the seaside: he missed his friends. Wendy promised to come again soon.

Apart from the emotional impact of reading about the birth itself, Wendy was struck by Mrs Shandy's determination to choose who should attend on the birth. And in the marriage contract specifying where her confinement should take place. Wendy assumed that the elder son had been born in London as Mrs Shandy had wished. She was intrigued by this practice of having detailed marriage contracts in which such things were laid down, and thought it would be a good idea if this was adopted today. Though now the contracts were more likely to be focussed on what should happen when the couple split up.

These old papers Alan had found were giving her much to think about. Religion had played such an important part in people's lives back then. She was moved by the sacrifices Trim and his family had to make to practise their Baptist faith. Her own parents were nominally Baptist, but neither she nor her parents attended chapel. Wendy's only connection was when she wrote 'Baptist' in the space on a form. Maybe she should find out what there was in the Baptist teachings that could have caused Trim's family to be so devoted, continuing to worship in spite of the oppression this brought.

Chapter Nine

The Captain and I spent our days on the bowling-green, where drawbridges, portcullises and gates were added. At *Christmas* the Captain, instead of a new suit of cloaths, which he always had, treated himself to a handsome sentry-box, for use in case of rain. This stood at the corner of the green where there was left a little kind of an esplanade, on this he and I would consider how best to proceed.

When the Captain received a plan of a town under siege, we enlarged the plan to the exact scale of the bowling-green, transferred the lines on the map to lines on the surface. To carry this out I used a large roll of pack thread and a number of small piquets, driving these into the ground at the several angles and redans. When these defences were completed, the constructions of the investing force were laid out. Their first parallel, to conform with the required distance from the defender's shot, often encroaching upon the kitchen garden, and being run up between rows of cabbages. But the town existed only on the paper of its plan.

'We could have a model town built for us,' I suggested, 'made from wood, painted and then placed within the polygon of the besiege works.'

The Captain was excited by my idea. 'We could have it in the style of those of which it was most representative,' he enthused, 'with grated windows, and the gable-ends of the houses facing the streets, as those in *Ghent* and *Bruges*.' The carpenter was set to work, with each house made to hook on or off to form any town we pleased. The Captain decided a church was needed and had made a fine one with a steeple. But when I suggested adding bells, he thought the metal would be best cast into cannons.

The Captain's aspirations for his modelled fortifications continued to grow, and it became his ambition to position artillery within them. My task, and much to my liking, was to construct these model field pieces as best I could. The first, being simple in design, were a couple of mortars I fashioned from a pair of old jack-boots I found at the *Hall*. Happy with the result of my ingenuity, I took the mortars to show the Captain, and found him and his brother asleep in the parlour.

'Pray what's the matter? Who is there? Cried Mr *Shandy*, waking the moment the door began to creak. '—I wish the smith would give a peep at that confounded hinge.' A comment I'd many times heard him make.

''Tis nothing,' I said, 'but two mortars I am bringing in to show...'

'If Dr *Slop* has any drugs to pound, let him do it in the kitchen.'

'They are two mortar pieces I have been making for a siege next summer,' I told him.

'My God, *Trim*, what has happened to my boots?' he cried, rising from his chair.

'Sir, they have become two siege-mortars. *Obadiah* said your honour had left off wearing them.'

'*Trim* has done this work for me,' the Captain now fully awake, said without hesitation.

'By heaven, *Toby*,' Mr *Shandy* exclaimed, 'I have not one appointment belonging to me which I set so much store by, as these jack-boots. They were our great-grandfather's, I declare I would not have taken ten pounds for them.'

'I'll pay you the money,' said the Captain, reaching into his breeches pocket, at the same time looking at the two mortars with infinite pleasure.

'They've been in the family since the civil wars—they are hereditary,' Mr *Shandy* lamented bitterly. 'Sir *Roger Shandy* wore them at the *Battle of Marston Moor*.'

Grandfather *Naylor* had also been at *Marston Moor* and told me how they had put the enemy to flight. In these boots Sir *Roger* would have been one of those fleeing Royalists, though this was not the occasion to speak of it. I don't know if the Captain ever gave his brother the ten pounds, but I doubt if it would have appeased Mr *Shandy*. The Captain coming quickly to my defence in the matter was typical of this honourable man.

The simulation of the bowling-green as a field of battle continued and was a constant feature of life at the Captain's house. The settled regularity of my life there was one day broken by the sudden arrival of *Susannah* in a dreadful state of distress.

'He is murdered—I will have to flee the country,' she wailed, and collapsed onto a chair. She sobbed out the story. She had been in the nursery with *Tristram* when the five-year old had want of the chamber pot, but the chamber-maid had not left one. The need appeared urgent, so with one hand *Susannah* lifted the child up onto the window seat, and with the other raised up the sash window to point the boy's male appendage out of the window. 'Slap came the sash down like lightning and chopped it clean off,' she wailed. 'Everywhere was blood.' The child screamed and *Susannah* had fled down the back stairs before his mother arrived. Passing the kitchen in her hurried escape to the sanctuary of our house, she had blurted out to the cook the reason for her flight. 'The whole house will now know,' she moaned.

My heart froze as her story unfolded, for I had played a part in this terrible maiming.

The Captain, in his eagerness to enact battle scenes within the model fortifications, required me to construct several model canons. When I ran out of lead for the casting of these, already having used parts of leaden downspouts and guttering, I utilised the weights from sash windows. There were insufficient of these in the house and some I took from the *Hall*. The Captain was delighted to have artillery at his disposal and began to conceive of a way to fire his cannons. It was my removal of the two sash weights in the nursery which had caused this calamity. And I it was who must bear the responsibility, and not *Susannah*. This I told her before going to recount to the Captain the whole sorry episode.

I found the Captain in the parlour with parson *Yorick*, and laid out the story of *Tristram's* tragedy, vowing that, as it was through my actions that it had occurred, I would not suffer *Susannah* to come to any harm in this matter.

'*Trim*,' said the Captain, 'if anything can be said to be a fault, when the service absolutely requires it should be done— 'tis I certainly who deserve the blame—you obeyed your orders.'

'Had Count *Solmes*, *Trim*,' said the parson, 'at the battle of *Solmes*, which has been the subject of our discussion, followed his King's orders, he would have saved thee being run over by a dragoon in the retreat.'

'And the five battalions who were cut down,' said the Captain. 'King *William* was so provoked by him disobeying his orders that he would not allow Count *Solmes* into his presence for several months.'

'I fear,' said the parson, 'that the squire will be as much provoked at the corporal as the King at the Count, yet he has behaved diametrically opposite to Count *Solmes* and may be rewarded with the same disgrace.'

'I would spring a mine,' cried the Captain, rising up, 'and blow up my fortifications and my house with them, perishing under the ruins, ere I would stand by and see it.'

He put on his hat and, accompanied by parson *Yorick*, with myself and *Susannah* following, led the way across to *Shandy Hall*.

'I wish instead of the sash-weights I had cut off the church spout,' I said, as we entered the door.

'You have cut off spouts enow,' said the parson.

Inside we found that the damage described by the grief-stricken *Susannah* had not been to the extent she had thought. 'A snip of skin off the end,' said Dr *Slop*. The young *Tristram* had been circumcised!

'Dear *Yorick*,' greeted Mr *Shandy*, when we went into the parlour. 'This *Tristram* of ours comes very hardly by all his religious rites. Never was the son of Jew, Christian, Turk, or Infidel initiated into them in so oblique and slovenly manner.'

'Is the child the worse for it?' the Captain asked.

'The Troglodytes say not,' said Mr *Shandy*. 'And theologians tell us he is the better for it.'

'Provided,' said *Yorick*, 'you travel him into *Egypt*.'

'He will have that advantage when he sees the Pyramids,' Mr *Shandy* said.

'Every word of this is Arabic to me,' said the Captain.

'*Ilus*,' continued Mr *Shandy*, 'is said to have circumcised his whole army one morning.'

'I know not by any article of war he could justify it,' said his brother.

We did not leave the *Hall* until the Captain had made it clear to his brother that the responsibility for the misadventure with the window, lay entirely on his shoulders.

Tristram's father, already having to reconcile himself to a misnamed son, and whose proud Shandyan nose had been damaged at birth, now had to contend with the fact of the child's unplanned circumcision. His response was to make a study of the history and practice of circumcision. When Mrs *Shandy* saw him with a couple of folios under his arm, and *Obadiah* following with a large reading desk, she took it for granted it was a herbal. 'Tell us what herbs will be needed,' she said. 'For that,' said her husband, 'you must send for Dr *Slop*.' His immediate concern being to settle in his mind whether the Jews copied the practice from the Egyptians, or the Egyptians from the Jews.

Dr *Slop* was engaged in applying his medical knowledge to the treatment of the child's injured member, assisted by an embarrassed *Susannah*. Her function, she told me, was to hold the candle whilst the Doctor tied a cataplasm onto the wound. She had expressed her reluctance to be present during this procedure, which had angered the Doctor. 'Come, come, Mrs

Modesty—if you won't hold the candle, and look, you may hold it and shut your eyes.'

'That's one of your popish shifts,' she said.

''Tis better than no shift at all,' he said, eyeing her bare arm.

'I defy you, Sir,' said *Susannah*, pulling the sleeve of her shift below her elbow.

In this hostile atmosphere Dr *Slop* snatched up the cataplasm, and *Susannah* snatched up the candle.

'A little this way,' he said.

Susannah looking one way, and manoeuvring the candle the other, set fire to the Doctor's wig.

'You impudent whore!' cried the Doctor.

'I never was the destruction of any body's nose,' shouted *Susannah*, 'which is more than you can say.'

Dr *Slop* responded by throwing the cataplasm in her face, and she replied in kind with what was left in the pan.

Chapter Ten

Thwarted in his intention of giving his son a fitting name, and his expectation that the child would bear a commanding Shanty nose forestalled by Dr *Slop's* forceps, Mr *Shandy* was determined to offset these defects by ensuring that the quality of the *Tristram's* upbringing and education would be the best that could be devised. To this end he read widely, studying the writings of recognised authorities on the subject. With the knowledge gained from his enquiries, adjusted to his own unique way of thinking, he announced his thoughts on the matter.

'*Tristram*,' he said, 'shall be made to conjugate every word in the dictionary, backwards and forwards the same way;— every word, *Yorick*, by this means, you see, is converted into a thesis or an hypothesis;—every thesis and hypothesis have an offspring of propositions:—and each proposition has its own consequences and conclusions; every one of which leads the mind on again, into fresh tracks of enquiries and doubtings.— The force of this engine,' he added, 'is incredible in opening a child's head.'

''Tis enough, brother *Shandy*,' cried the Captain, 'to burst it into a thousand splinters.'

'I presume,' said parson *Yorick*, smiling, 'it must be owing to this that the famous *Vincent Quirino* should be able to paste up in the publick schools at *Rome*, so early as the eighth year of his age, no less than four thousand, five hundred, and sixty different theses, upon the most abstruse points of the most abstruse theology.'

'What is that,' said Mr *Shandy*, 'to what is told us of *Alphonsus Tastatus*, who, almost in his nurse's arms, learned all the sciences and liberal arts without being taught any of them.'

Mr *Shandy* and the parson continued, each attempting to outdo the other by citing evermore outrageous examples of the learned abilities of young children. The matter was brought to a head when the parson spoke of 'the great *Lipsius* who composed a work the day he was born.'

'They should have wiped it up,' said the Captain.

Ignoring his brother's remark, Mr *Shandy* continued to speak of his plans for *Tristram*.

''Tis high time to take this young creature out of women's hands, and put him into to those of a private governor. Now as I consider the person who is to be about my son, as the mirror in which he is to view himself morning to night, and by which he is to adjust his looks, his carriage, and perhaps the inmost sentiments of his heart,—I would have one, *Yorick*, if possible, polished at all points, fit for my child to look into.'

'This is very good sense,' said the Captain.

'There is,' his brother continued, 'a certain mien and motion of the body and all its parts, both in acting and speaking, which argues a man well within. There are a thousand unnoticed openings which let at once a penetrating eye into a man's soul. A man of sense does not lay down his hat in coming into a room,—or take it up in going out of it, but something escapes, which discovers him. It is for these reasons that the governor I make choice of; *shall neither lisp, or squint, or wink, or talk loud, or look fierce, or foolish,—or bite his lips, or grind his teeth, or speak through his nose, or pick it, or blow it with his fingers.—*

He shall neither walk fast,—or slow, or fold his arms,—for that is laziness,—or hang them down,—for that is folly, or hide them in his pocket, for that is nonsense.—

He shall neither strike, or pinch, or tickle,—or bite, or cut his nails, or hawk, or spit, or snift, or drum with his feet or fingers in company,—nor (according to *Erasmus*) shall he speak to anyone in making water,—nor shall he point to carrion or excrement.'

'This is all nonsense,' the Captain said, but his brother was undeterred, adding to his requirements of a governor for his son: the man should be; cheerful, jovial, prudent, attentive to business, vigilant, acute, inventive, wise, judicious and learned.

'And why not humble, and gentle tempered, and good?' said parson *Yorick*.

'And why not,' said the Captain, 'free, and generous, and bountiful, and brave?'

'He shall, my dear *Toby*,' said Mr *Shandy*, getting up and shaking his brother by the hand.

7

Alan was surprised that a meeting like the one at Putney described by Corporal Trim, could have taken place so long ago. It made him curious to know more about what the Agitators were proposing: his mother had spoken of his father being 'an agitator'.

'Do you think there will be anything on the internet about an old pamphlet called 'The Agreement of the People?' he asked Wendy.

'I'll see what I can find,' she said, expecting that this would be about an aspect of *The Corporal's Story* she had not yet come across. She knew from his bookmark that Alan was further into the book than she, who kept her own reading discreet by noting the number of the page she had reached.

In his progress through Trim's account Alan began to think about his own family history, though the hope of making money from his discovery continued to be his main concern. Wendy seemed to have softened in her attitude to the cottage, no longer protesting about the time he spent on it. Was she coming round to the idea of going to live there? But the money had practically run out, soon he would have to leave off the renovation and look for paid employment. This was clouding his thoughts on his way to another day at the cottage.

'I've found that pamphlet you asked about,' Wendy greeted him, when he came in that evening.

'Oh, good—thanks, I'll have a look at it when I've got some food in me.

An Agreement of the Free People of England, Alan read from the document on the screen. He saw that Lieutenant Colonel

John Lilburne was one the four authors, all of whom were prisoners in the Tower of London —*From our causelesse captivity in the Tower*—when they issued this manifesto on May 1st 1649. John Lilburne was a name Trim had mentioned, his grandfather describing him as being one of the Agitators in the New Model Army. Was this the reason for him being imprisoned? Alan didn't think any prisoner today would be allowed to issue a political manifesto during their time inside.

He read, in language little different from that he was becoming familiar with in Trim's writings, that the supreme authority in England *shall be and reside henceforth in a Representative of the People consisting of four hundred persons.* Most men over twenty-one would have the right to vote in their selection of *the said four hundred Members proportionable to the respective parts of the Nation.* An election would be held every twelve months. Much of the manifesto was taken up with the necessary safeguards to ensure the continuing existence of this new constitution.

'This must have been revolutionary stuff back then,' said Alan.

Chapter Eleven

Not since his army days had the Captain, unlike his brother, been much concerned with the health of others. This changed suddenly when the young lieutenant *Le Fever*, who was not of any kin to the *Shandy* family, came to his attention one summer evening. The landlord of a little inn in the village came into the parlour where the Captain and I were sitting at supper. The landlord had with him an empty phial and wished to beg a glass or two of sack.

''Tis for a poor gentleman—I think, of the army,' he said, 'who has been taken ill at my house four days ago, and has never held up his head since, or had a desire to taste anything till just now, and has a fancy for a glass of sack and a thin toast. I could neither beg, borrow or buy such a thing, I would almost steal it for the poor gentleman—he is so ill. I hope to God he will still mend—we are all of us concerned for him.'

'Thou art a good natured soul,' cried the Captain, 'and thou shall drink the poor gentleman's health in a glass of sack thyself, and take a couple of bottles with my service, and tell him he is heartily welcome to them—and to a dozen more if they will do him good.'

'Though I am persuaded he is a very compassionate fellow,' said the Captain, as the landlord shut the door, 'yet I cannot help entertaining a high opinion of his guest too. There must be something more than common in him, that in so short a time, should win so much on the affection of his host.'

'And of the whole family,' I said, 'for they are all concerned for him.'

The Captain was keen to know the name of the sick man, but the landlord, when I caught up with him, said he had quite forgotten it, and would ask the man's son, a boy of about eleven or twelve years. 'The poor creature has tasted almost as little as his father. He does nothing but mourne and lament for him night and day, and has not stirred from the bedside these two days.'

The Captain was deeply affected when I told him of the boy, laying down his knife and fork, and thrusting his plate from him.

'*Trim*,' he said, 'I have a mind to visit this poor gentlemen.'

'It is a cold and rainy night, and likely to bring on the torment in your groin,' I said. 'Let me go and reconnoitre, and bring you a full account.'

An hour later I was back at the house and telling the Captain of lieutenant *Le Fever's* condition.

'An army man—an officer,' said the Captain.

'After a glass of sack he was sufficiently revived to see me. I told him of your extreme concern and that he was heartily welcome to anything in Captain *Shandy's* house or cellar.'

'Thou could have added my purse too,' said the Captain.

'He expressed his thanks to you for your courtesy in offering him your help. He was returning from *Ireland* to his regiment in *Flanders* when taken ill and unable to proceed. The hired horses were paid off and his purse was empty. He is in *Angus's* regiment and says he knew of you when his regiment fought alongside *Leven's* regiment in *Flanders*. Tell Captain *Shandy*, he said, I was the ensign at *Breda* whose wife was unfortunately killed with a musket shot as she lay in my arms in my tent.'

'I remember well the story, *Trim*, the circumstances of the incident inciting pity throughout the whole regiment.'

'When I wished the young man goodnight he rose from his bed and saw me to the bottom of the stairs. The youth came into the kitchen to order the thin toast for his father—but I will do it for my father myself, he said.'

'Pray let me save you the trouble, said I, taking up a fork for the purpose, and offering him my chair by the fire, whilst I did it. I believe, Sir, said he, I can please him best myself. I am sure said I, his honour will not like the toast the worse for being toasted by an old soldier.—The youth took hold of my hand and instantly burst into tears.'

'Poor youth!' said the Captain, 'he has been bred up from an infant in the army, and the name of a soldier, *Trim*, sounded in his ears like the name of a friend. A sick brother officer should have the best quarters, and if we had him with us we could tend and look after him. Thou art an excellent nurse thyself, *Trim*, and what with thy care of him, and the boy's and mine together, we might recruit him again at once and set him upon his legs. In a fortnight or three week he might march.'

'He will never march in this world,' I said.

'He will march,' insisted the Captain.

'To his grave,' I said. 'The landlord told me he heard the death watch all night long.'

'He shall march to his regiment,' said the Captain. 'He shall be supported.'

'We shall do what we can for him—but the poor soul will die.'

'He shall not die, by God,' cried the Captain.

In the morning I went to get a physician and the Captain visited lieutenant *Le Fever* to tell him that he was to be cared for at the Captain's home. When he returned from the inn he was in deep distress. 'What will happen to the boy?' were the only words that came from him. In a little while he spoke of having informed the lieutenant that he would be moved to the Captain's house.

'He looked up wistfully at my face—then cast a look upon his boy. And I watched as the lieutenant's life edged away.'

For me the death was not unexpected, but the Captain was distraught.

'I will see to the care of the boy—and for his education,' he said, and seemed to gain solace from this thought. *Billy*, for that was the boy's, name was taken into the Captain's household. The Captain, with the boy in his hand, attended lieutenant *Le Fever's* funeral as chief mourners. Parson *Yorick* preached a funeral service over the lieutenant, whom he honoured by burying him in the chancel. After settling all *Le Fever's* accounts with the agent of the regiment there remained nothing more than an old regimental coat and a sword. The coat the Captain gave to me. 'Wear it, *Trim*, as long as it will hold together, for the sake of the poor lieutenant.'

He drew the sword from the scabbard and hung it on a crook.

'This I'll save for thee,' he said to *Le Fever's* son. ''Tis all the fortune, my dear boy, which God has left thee, but he has given thee a heart to fight thy way with it in the world.'

After some basic lessons from the Captain, *Billy* went to a public school where, excepting *Whitsontide* and *Christmas,* when he returned to us, he remained until the spring of the year, seventeen. Fired by stories of the emperor sending his army into *Hungary* against the Turks, he left his Greek and Latin without leave, and came to beg the Captain for his sword, and his leave along with it, to go and try his fortune under *Prince Eugene.* The Captain's excitement was such as to bring on pain to his wound. 'I would go with thee, if I were able,' he said, sorrowfully, his hand upon his groin. Then he took down the sword from where it had hung untouched ever since the lieutenant's death, and put it into the young man's hand. He detained young *Le Fever* for a fortnight, during which time he ensured the prospective soldier was fully equipped, and a contract for his passage to *Leghorn* obtained.

Young *Le Fever* got up to the Imperial army just time enough to try what metal his sword was made of at the defeat of the Turks before *Belgrade.* But a series of mischances pursued him in the years that followed. The last contact was by letter in which he said he had lost his health, and everything but his sword. He was at *Marseilles* in poor health and waiting for a ship in which to return. I wondered if he would ever again be with us.

8

'Don't bother to make a meal tonight,' Alan said, suddenly, as he was about to leave for the cottage, 'we'll go out to a restaurant.'

'That will be nice,' said Wendy, 'I'm ready for a change.'

Much of her social life was on the internet, and, apart from an occasional trip out with a local heritage group, her social contacts were mainly on the laptop. Though she had recently begun attending an evening class in cookery, and the experience had made her think about other classes. She didn't consider herself to be the social type, not like Maureen at work, always talking about something she had been to, or somewhere she was going. Wendy had no contact with her away from work, where, apart from her asking about Alan, little was ever said about the Norwegian cruise.

It was an impulsive act, suggesting they go out for a meal, not something Alan had thought about before the words came out. But what the hell—whilst he still had some money. And once said he realised he needed a break from what had become a fixed routine, working alone at the cottage each day, and slumping in front of the telly in the evening. The one change was that he now also read the manuscript for an hour or so.

They went to Howard's, a restaurant Wendy suggested having heard Maureen speak well of it—'proper English food,' she had said. Each of them had put on their best for the outing, Alan even wearing a tie. At the restaurant Wendy felt stiff and awkward, Alan too was subdued. Seen in a large mirror as they stood waiting together for their table, they looked as rigid as a wedding photograph.

Wendy decided on the roast lamb and new potatoes, Alan went for steak and chips.

'What would you like to drink?' he said.

'I don't know—perhaps a glass of white wine.'

For himself he ordered a beer. Neither said much as they waited to be served. Wendy began to wonder why they were here. She relaxed once she'd had a mouthful of wine, and the food was on the table. Alan watched her, thinking how great she looked, with her hair done, and wearing make-up that made her look younger. He'd been aware that she'd started taking more care over her appearance, but he hadn't before realised just how attractive she was. His eyes went over the other diners in the restaurant, at the other partnered women eating there, and was happy with the thought that there would be men there envious of him.

'Have another glass,' he said, and from the way Alan looked at her Wendy had the startling thought that he was going to propose. What would she say if he did? Could she trust Alan enough to be tied to him? The shock of betrayal by her former husband still weighed on her mind.

'I need to find some work,' he said. 'The money's run out for the cottage.' Wendy's immediate reaction was relief that she was not going to be asked to make a decision about marriage; matters of money easier to answer. But the expected question of finance did not come, Alan's statement of fact was not followed by a request for money. She looked at him and he held her gaze; if he had proposed at that moment she would have said yes.

'I'd like to come and see how you're getting on with the cottage,' she said, and his eyes were bright with hope.

Chapter Twelve

The Captain asked me to fetch his copy of the book by *Stevinus*, that great mathematician and engineer. Not required on this occasion for the book's authoritative passages on fortifications, but for details of the celebrated sailing chariot invented by *Stevinus*, and was of such wonderful contrivance and velocity as to carry half-a-dozen people thirty German miles. When I returned with the book, Dr *Slop*, who had joined the Captain and his brother, said that I could have been spared the trouble as on his return from *Leyden* he had gone to *Schevling* where he saw the sailing chariot.

'But pray, Dr *Slop*,' said Mr *Shandy*, 'upon what principles was this self-same chariot set a-going?'

'Upon very pretty principles to be sure,' said the Doctor, 'and I have often wondered why none of our Gentry, who live on large plains like this of ours, attempt nothing of this kind. It would be excellent good husbandry to make use of the winds, which cost nothing, and which eat nothing, rather than horses, which both cost and eat a great deal.'

'For that very reason,' said Mr *Shandy*. 'Because they cost nothing and eat nothing—the scheme is bad—it is the consumption of our products, as well as the manufactures of them, which gives bread to the hungry, circulates trade—brings in money, and supports the value of our lands. Tho' I own, if I was a Prince, I would generously recompense the scientific head which brought forth such contrivances;—yet I would as peremptorily suppress the use of them.'

'You may take *Stevinus* home again, *Trim*,' the Captain said.

'But pri'thee, *Trim*,' said Mr *Shandy*, 'first look into it and see if thou can'st spy aught of a sailing chariot in it.'

In opening the book out fell some sheets of paper, which I picked up from the floor.

'It has the appearance of a sermon,' I said.

'I cannot conceive how such a thing as a sermon could have got into my *Stevinus*,' the Captain said.

'I have ever a strong propensity,' said Mr *Shandy*, 'to look into things which cross my way by such strange fatalities as these. Are you able to read out a page or two?'

'*Trim* can read it as well as I can,' said the Captain.

I had officiated two whole campaigns in *Flanders*, as Clerk to the Chaplain of the Regiment. I stood before them, and began.

'Hebrews, chapter thirteen, verse eighteen. For we trust we have a good conscience. Trust!—Trust we have a good conscience!'

'*Trim*, you give that sentence a very improper accent,' interrupted Mr *Shandy*, 'for you curl up your nose, and read it with such a sneering tone, as if the parson was going to abuse the Apostle.'

'He is,' I said.

'*Trim* is certainly in the right,' said Dr *Slop*, 'for the writer, who I perceive is a Protestant by the snappish manner in which he takes up the Apostle, is certainly going to abuse him.'

'From whence,' said Mr *Shandy*, 'have you concluded so soon, Dr *Slop*, the writer is of our Church?—for aught I can see yet,—he may be of any Church.'

There followed a lengthy discussion regarding the differences between their Churches, and mention was made of the Inquisition, a name which set my heart throbbing for my poor brother held within its clutches.

'Come, *Trim*,' said Mr *Shandy*, 'read on—I have a great desire to know what kind of provocation the Apostle has given.'

I continued to read the sermon, interrupted occasionally by comments from my listeners.

'The language is good, and I declare *Trim* reads very well,' said Mr *Shandy*.

It proved to be a lengthy sermon, but the interruptions, which came mainly from Dr *Slop* wishing to state the view of his Church, lessened after he fell asleep. Finally I came to the end.

'Thou hast read the sermon extremely well, *Trim*,' said Mr *Shandy*. 'I see plainly that it has been composed to be preach'd at the Temple,—or at some Assize.'

'But pray,' said the Captain, 'whose can this be?'

'Unless my judgement greatly deceives me,—I know the author, for 'tis wrote, certainly, by the parson of the parish,' said his brother.

'Our *Yorick*?'

'The similitude of the stile and manner of it, is that which I hear constantly preach'd in his parish church.'

'*Yorick* did borrow my *Stevinus*. The parson is inquisitive of all manner of things.'

'He must have popp'd the sermon into the book as soon as it was finished, and, by an act of forgetfulness, to which he was ever subject, he had sent *Stevinus* home, and his sermon to keep him company,' said Mr *Shandy*.

The source of the sermon was proved beyond doubt the next day, a servant coming from the parson to enquire after it.

Despite my delivery of the sermon being much praised, and he not present, in his book *Tristram* makes sly fun of my reading of it.

He stood before them with his body swayed, and bent forwards just so far, as to make an angle of 85 degrees and a half upon the plain of the horizon—which sound orators, to whom I address this know very well to be the true persuasive angle of incidence... How the duce Corporal Trim, who knew not so much as an acute angle from an obtuse one, came to hit it so accurately...To complete the picture, he stood with his right leg firm under him, the foot of his left leg, the defect of which was no disadvantage to his attitude, advanced a little... So much for Corporal Trim's body and legs. He held the sermon loosely—not carelessly, in his left hand, raised something above his stomach, and detached a little from his breast—his right arm falling negligently by his side, as nature and the laws of gravity ordered it.

Chapter Thirteen

The letter came when I was with the Captain in the parlour at the *Hall*. *Walter Shandy*, with a map and a book of post roads, was busy calculating the expense of riding post from *Calais* to *Paris* and on to *Lyons*. Believing that no gentlemen's education was complete without having toured *Europe*, he planned to spend the legacy from aunt *Dinah* on such a tour for *Robert*. He had got almost to the end of his calculations when *Obadiah* opened the door to acquaint him that the family was out of yeast. 'Might I take the great coach horse early in the morning and ride in search of some?' he asked.

'With all my heart—take the coach horse, and welcome.' said Mr *Shandy*, turning again to his task.

Obadiah returned a few minutes later. 'He wants a shoe, poor creature.'

'Then ride the Scotch horse,' Mr *Shandy* said hastily.

'He cannot bear a saddle on his back, for the whole world,' said *Obadiah*. 'The devil's in that horse.'

'Then take *Patriot*—and shut the door.'

'*Patriot* is sold,' said *Obadiah*. 'Your worship ordered me to sell him last April.'

'Then go on foot for your pains.'

'I had much rather walk than ride,' *Obadiah* said, shutting the door.

Mr *Shandy* resumed his calculations, and, pre-occupied with the book of French post roads, he gestured to his brother to open the letter that had been brought in. Groans came from the Captain as he read.

'Gone,' he announced.

'Where?—who?' said his brother.

'My poor nephew.'

'What—without leave—without money—without governor?' cried *Walter Shandy* in amazement.

'He is dead, dear brother,' the Captain said.

"Without being ill?'

'I dare say not,' said the Captain, in a low voice, fetching a deep sigh from the bottom of his heart.

After expressing my grief over this sad news, I left the brothers seeking consolation together. I knew little of *Tristram's* older brother, who seldom visited the *Hall*. Apart from the news of his death, *Robert* is surprisingly absent in his brother's book, and in which *Tristram* shows no emotional response to the news.

Stepping into the kitchen later that day, I found *Susannah* in tears. 'Here is sad news, *Trim*,' she cried. 'Master *Bobby* is dead.'

'Yes,' I said.

'It is true,' said *Obadiah*, 'I heard the letter read.'

At *Shandy Hall*, and probably in most similar households, the staff was well informed of what was going on in the family. Doors were never firmly closed by servants, allowing sufficient space for secrets to find closely attentive ears.

'I lament for him from my heart and my soul,' I said.

'O! 'twill be the death of my poor mistress,' *Susannah* said, wiping her eyes. 'We shall all have to go into mourning.'

'He was alive last *Whitsontide*,' said *Jonathan*, the coachman.

Jonathan's comment roused me to address those gathered in the kitchen, on the fragility of life.

'Are we not here now,' I said, striking my stick firmly upon the ground, to give an idea of sound health. 'And are we not gone—in a moment,' letting my hat fall upon the ground. *Susannah* burst into a flood of tears. *Obadiah*, the cook, *Jonathan*, the maid, and the scullion, who left off scouring a fish kettle, all seemed to melt and crowd around me.

'To us, *Jonathan*, who, being in the service of the best of masters, know not what want or care is, the time since *Whitsontide* is as nothing, but to those who know what death is, and what havock and destruction it can make before a man can well wheel about—'tis like a whole age. It would make a good-natured man's heart bleed to consider how many brave and upright fellows have been laid low since that time. And trust me *Suzy*,' I said, turning to *Susannah*, whose eyes were swimming in water, 'before *Whitsontide* comes round again, many a bright eye will be dim. Are we not like a flower of the field—is not all flesh grass? 'Tis clay—'tis dirt.'

'I could hear *Trim* talk so for ever,' cried *Susannah*, laying her hand on my shoulder.

I was beginning to sound more like the chaplain than myself. Before I became a soldier I had considered a life of religion within the Baptist circuit, and had often spoken at chapel meetings.

A recent memory of the attraction this had for me, had come when I stood reading out the sermon that had dropped out of the Captain's copy of *Stevinus*.

'In battle I value death not this much,' and snapped my fingers. 'What is he, Death? A pull of the trigger—a push of a bayonet, an inch this way or that. I have looked him in the face a hundred times and know what Death is, and could I escape him by creeping into the worse calf's skin that ever was made into a knapsack, I would do it there—but that is nature.'

'Nature is nature,' said *Jonathan*.

'And that is the reason,' cried *Susannah*, 'I so much pity my mistress—she will never get over it.'

'I pity the Captain the most of any one in the family,' I said. 'Madam will get ease of heart by weeping—the Squire in talking about it—but the poor Captain will keep it all in silence to himself. When lieutenant *Le Fever* died I heard him sigh in his bed for a whole month together. "You sigh so piteously," I said to him.

"I cannot help it, *Trim*," he answered, "'tis so melancholy a death—I cannot get it off my heart."

"Yet you fear not death yourself."

"I hope, *Trim,*" he said, "I fear nothing but the doing of a wrong thing." '

'I like to hear *Trim's* stories about the Captain,' said *Susannah*.

'He is a kindly-hearted gentleman,' said *Obadiah*.

'And as a brave a one too, as ever stepped before a platoon,' I said. 'He would march up to the mouth of a cannon though he saw the lighted match at the very touch-hole. Yet he has a heart as soft as a child for other people.'

'I would sooner drive such a gentleman for seven pounds a year—than some for eight,' said *Jonathan*.

'He is a friend and brother to me,' I told them.

*

Tristram did not make fun of my oration in the kitchen, in which I used my stick and hat to drive home the message, as he had with my reading of the sermon. But drew from it a warning of the threat of such eloquence.

Now as I perceive plainly, that the preservation of our constitution in church and state,—and possibly the preservation of the whole world—or what is the same thing, the distribution and balance of its property and power, may in time to come to depend greatly on the right understanding of this stroke of the corporal's eloquence—I do demand your attention,—your worships and reverences...

...Ye who govern this mighty world and its mighty concerns with the engines of eloquence,—who heat it, and cool it, and melt it, and mollify it,—and then harden it again to your purpose—

Ye who wind and turn the passions with this great windlass,—and, having done it, lead the owners of them, whither ye think meet—

Ye, lastly, who drive—and why not, Ye also who are driven, like turkeys to market, with a stick and red clout—meditate—meditate, I beseech you, upon Trim's hat.

His observation stirred within me those silenced hopes of the *New Jerusalem* that grandfather *Naylor* had spoken of.

*

'My brother,' the Captain told me, 'has a strong belief in the philosophical approach to the troubles of life, and turning to philosophy his way of dealing with the grief arising from the loss of his son.'

'I know of no philosophy which would prevent me shedding a single tear,' I said.

'Nor I,' said the Captain, 'yet my brother remained dry-eyed as he spoke of the inevitability of the passing of life. Monarchs and princes dance in the same ring with us, he said, and went on at length about cities and civilisations, famous in history, but no longer existing, and all manner of views and philosophies concerning death. The Thracians wept when a child was born, he said, and feasted and made merry when a man went out of the world. None of what he spoke of was convincing to me, but my brother seemed to find much ease from it.'

The Captain recounted the numerous examples his brother cited of the occurrence of death in classical times. One anecdote was of the death of *Cornelius Gallus*, the praetor, who died whilst lying in bed with a woman. 'If it was with his wife there could be no hurt in it,' I told my brother. 'That's more than I know,' was his reply.

Tristram expresses no personal feelings over the death of his brother. He uses the occasion of his father hearing of the death of his eldest son, and his reaction to the news, as an opportunity for a blatant display of his own learning.

'Tis either Plato, or Plutarch, or Seneca, or Xenophon, or Epictetus, or Theophrastus, or Lucien—or someone perhaps of later date—either Cardan, or Budaeus, or Petrarch, or Stella—or possibly some divine or father of the church, St Austin, or St Cyprian, or Barnard, who affirms that it is an irresistible and natural passion to weep for the loss of our friends or children—and Seneca (I'm positive) tells us somewhere, that such griefs evacuate themselves best by that particular channel. And accordingly we find that David wept for his son Absolom—Adrian for

his Antinous—Niobe for her children, and that Apollodorus and Crito both shed tears for Socrates before his death.

My father managed his affliction otherwise; and indeed different from most men either ancient or modern; for he neither wept it away, as the Hebrews and the Romans—or slept it off, as the Laplanders—or hang'd it as the English, or drowned it, as the Germans—nor did he curse it, or damn it, or excommunicate it. He got rid of it, however.

9

Riding with Alan in the cab of his pickup gave Wendy a feeling of partnership, pleased that she had suggested this visit to the cottage. 'There's still quite a bit to do,' he said, worried that its unfinished state would kill the unexpected interest she was showing. He glanced apprehensively at the sky, at clouds moving towards the sun, threatening the bright day he had hoped for. They arrived in the village and he pulled into the space in front of the cottage. 'This will be the front garden,' he explained, as they got out onto the compacted surface. Wendy stood scrutinising the building which no longer had the derelict look she remembered, the windows repaired and the broken guttering replaced. She cast her eyes around the surrounding houses; across the road a woman watched them from behind a window.

'The external work is practically finished,' Alan said. His concern was that she would be put off by what she saw inside, especially the state of the kitchen. He unlocked the front door with a large, ancient-looking key, and they went in. The musty old carpets had gone, the air fresher than when she was here before. Everywhere were signs of Alan's work, walls and ceilings newly plastered, central heating radiators installed, new floorboards fitted. 'A lot of the work has been in the roof,' he said. They went through into the kitchen.

'This is where the units will go,' he began, but Wendy's interest was elsewhere, gazing out of the window to the area behind the cottage.

'Those old trees could be what's left of the yew hedge,' she said, excitement in her voice.

Alan stared at her. 'So, you're reading it too—I thought as much.' His hopes soaring by what he was hearing.

'Yes—before you come home. This cottage could be where the corporal lived.'

'Trim and the Captain—I've thought so too,' he said, dizzied by this possibility.

'And that ridge,' she said.

He looked where she pointed, to a raised grassy line that ran up to the wooden fencing of a modern bungalow. 'Yes— could be the remains of one of Trim's fortifications.'

'How much will it take to finish the work?'

'I need a drink,' he said.

They sat in a quiet corner of the village pub, he with a half-pint—'driving' he told the bar woman, as if ordering half a pint needed an explanation. Wendy had coffee, alcohol not for her at this time of day.

'At least eight thousand, maybe more—it depends.'

'Depends on what?'

'Whether it's done for sale or...'

'Or?'

'For us,' his eyes fixed on his empty glass.

Wendy was silent, sipping the last of her coffee. 'There's a lot to think about,' she said finally.

'There is,' he agreed, his eyes lifting from the beer glass to look at her.

'Do you know if widow Wadman gets Captain Shandy?' she said.

'I'll not spoil the story for you,' Alan smiling now.

They left the pub and walked in warm sun through the village to the cottage.

'Don't look for a job yet,' she said.

Chapter Fourteen

Walter Shandy's concern with health became more pronounced after his son died when still a young man. 'O blessed health,' he was heard to say, 'thou art above all gold and treasure.' In true fashion he had read widely about health and longevity, leading to him formulating an hypothesis on the subject.

'The whole secret of health,' he said to parson *Yorick*, 'depending upon the due contention for mastery betwixt the radical heat and the radical moisture.'

'You have proved that to be a matter of fact, I suppose,' said the parson.

'Sufficiently,' was the reply, and he criticised *Francis Bacon*, whose English name *Tristram* discards in his account favouring a classical language, and uses the scientist's title *Veralam*. 'He held,' continued Mr *Shandy*, 'that the two great causes which conspire to shorten life are, the internal spirit, which like a gentle flame, wastes the body down to death, and secondly, the external air that parches the body up to ashes.'

The Captain, always eager to talk of sieges, took the opportunity of his brother's talk of radical heat and radical moisture, to bring up the topic of the siege of *Limerick*.

'Corporal *Trim* and I,' he said, 'had all along a burning fever, attended with a most raging thirst, otherwise what you call the radical moisture, must, as I conceive it, inevitably have got the better. It was heaven's mercy to us which put it in *Trim's* head to maintain that contention you speak of, by reinforcing the fever with hot wine and spices, whereby the radical heat stood its ground against the moisture.'

His brother drew in his lungs top full of air, and looking up, blew it forth again, as slowly as he possibly could. Hearing his brother tarnish the radical hypothesis by presenting an inapplicable example from his time at *Limerick*, Mr *Shandy* seemed as if he were going to explode.

Parson *Yorick*, knowing the signs, averted a possible outburst by asking me what was my opinion concerning this self-same radical heat and radical moisture.

'Speak they opinion freely,' said the Captain.

My concern was to avoid contributing to an argument between the brothers, and I decided to mount a diversionary manoeuvre. I was about to speak when in walked Dr *Slop*, greeted affably by Mr *Shandy*, whose changes of mood were unaccountably sudden. He satisfied himself about the Doctor's visit to the *Hall* and then said: 'Let the corporal go on with his medical lecture.' And I began by describing the saturated conditions at the siege, the Captain adding that *Limerick* was quite surrounded with the *Shannon*, and one of the strongest fortified places in *Ireland*. 'I think this is a new fashion,' said Dr *Slop*, 'of beginning a medical lecture.'

I continued by explaining how I kept the inside of the tent dry by burning a dish of brandy each night.

'And what conclusion dost thou draw, corporal *Trim*, from this experience?' said Mr *Shandy*.

'I knew nothing of radical moisture or radical heat, but learnt much about ditch water and of burning brandy, the heat of one counteracting the damp of the other.'

Tristram, as on numerous other occasions, distorts this scene, describing my behaviour in ways which accord with his characterisation of me in his book as a simple, uneducated person, lacking in any deeper sensibility.

Chapter Fifteen

The *Treaty of Utrecht* in 1713 ended the *War of Spanish Succession* and brought to an end *Louis XIV's* attempt to establish French dominance in *Europe*. It also curtailed the Captain's pleasure on the bowling-green of re-creating *Marborough's* campaigns.

'Never mind, brother *Toby*,' said *Walter Shandy*, always ready to mock the Captain's "hobby horse", 'by God's blessing we shall have another war break out some of these days; and when it does, the belligerent powers, if they would hang themselves, cannot keep us out of play. I defy 'em, my dear *Toby*, to take countries without taking towns—or towns without sieges.'

The Captain made no immediate reply, but by the way he lay down his pipe I knew that he was aggrieved by his brother's ungenerous comments. I have with me to this day the Captain's written response—his apological oration.

I am not insensible, brother Shandy, that when a man, whose profession is arms, wishes, as I have done, for war,—it has an ill aspect to the world;—and that, how just and right soever his motives and intentions may be,—he stands in an uneasy posture in vindicating himself from private views in doing it.

For this cause, if a soldier is a prudent man, which he may be, without being a jot the less brave, he will be sure not to utter his wish in the hearing of an enemy, for say what he will, an enemy will not believe him.—He will be cautious of doing it even to a friend,—lest he may suffer in esteem:—But if his heart is overcharged, and a secret sigh for arms must have its vent, he will reserve it for the ear of a brother, who knows his character to the bottom, and what his true notions, dispositions, and principles of honour are: What, I hope, I have been in all these, brother Shandy, would be unbecoming of me to say:—much worse, I know, have I been than I ought,—and something worse, perhaps, than I think. But much as I am, you, my dear brother Shandy, who have sucked the same breasts with me,—and with whom I have been brought up from my cradle,—and from whom knowledge, from the first hours of our boyish pastimes, down to this, I have concealed no one action of my life, and scarce a thought in it—Such as I am, brother, you must by this time know me, with all my vices, and with all my weaknesses too, whether of my age, my temper, my passions, or my understanding.

Tell me then, my dear brother Shandy, upon which of them it is, that when I condemned the peace of Utrecht, and grieved the war was not carried on with vigour a little longer, you should think your brother should do it upon unworthy views; or that in wishing for war, he should be bad enough to wish more of his fellow creatures slain,—more slaves made, and more families driven from their peaceful habitations, merely for his own pleasure:—Tell me, brother Shandy, upon which one deed of mine do you ground it?

If, when I was a school-boy, I could not hear a drum beat, but my heart beat with it—was it my fault?—Did I plant the propensity there?—did I sound the alarm within, or Nature?

When Guy, Earl of Warwick, and Parismus, and Parismenus, and Valentine and Orson, and The Seven Champions of England were handed round at school,—were they not all purchased with my own pocket money? Was that selfish, brother Shandy? When we read over the siege of Troy, which lasted ten years and eight months,—though with such a train of artillery as we had at Namur, the town might have been carried in a week—was I not as much concerned for the destruction of the Greeks and Trojans as any boy in the whole school? Had I not three strokes of a ferula given me, two on my right hand, and one on my left, for calling Helena a bitch for it? Did any one of you shed more tears for Hector? And when king Priam came to the camp to beg his body, and returned weeping back to Troy without it,—you know, brother, I could not eat my dinner.

Did that bespeak me cruel? Or because, brother Shandy, my blood flew out into the camp, and my heart panted for war,—was it proof it could not ache for the distresses of war too?

O brother! 'tis one thing for a soldier to gather laurels,—and 'tis another to scatter cypress.—'Tis one thing, brother Shandy, to hazard his own life—to leap first down into the trench, where he is sure to be cut to pieces:—'Tis one thing, from public spirit and a thirst for glory, to enter the breach the first man,—to stand in the foremost rank, and march bravely on with drums and trumpets, and colours flying about his ears:— 'Tis one thing, I say, brother Shandy, to do this—and 'tis another thing to reflect on the miseries of war;—to view the desolations of whole countries, and consider the intolerable fatigues which the soldier himself, the instrument who works them is forced (for six pence a day, if he can get it) to undergo.

Need I be told, dear Yorick, as I was by you, in Le Fever's funeral service, 'That so soft and gentle a creature, born to love, to mercy, and kindness, as man is, was not shaped for this?'—But why did you not add, Yorick,—if not by NATURE—that he is so by NECESSITY?—For what is war? What is it, Yorick, when fought as ours has been, upon principles of liberty of honour—what is it but the getting together of quiet and harmless people, with their swords in their hands, to keep the ambitious and the turbulent within bounds? And heaven is my witness, brother Shandy that the pleasure I have taken in these things,—and that infinite delight, in particular, which has attended my sieges in my bowling green, has aroused within me, and I hope in the corporal too, from the consciousness we both had, that in carrying them on, we were answering the great ends of our creation.

It was unusual in arguments with his brother for the Captain to go to such lengths, and, as was often the case, *Walter Shandy* would base his arguments on philosophies and learned tracts unknown to the Captain, who was likely to whistle the tune of Lillibullero, his usual response when anything shocked or surprised him, but especially when anything he deemed absurd was offered. The Captain got this habit in *Ireland* where *King William's* soldiers took to mocking the Irish Catholic Jacobins in satirical verses sung to the tune of Lillibullero.

A running disagreement between the brothers was their different attitudes to their aunt *Dinah*, who, pregnant with his child, had married her coachman. Mr *Shandy* regularly referred to the situation of their aunt, but the Captain could not bear to be reminded of this family disgrace. 'For God's sake,' he would say, 'and for my sake, and for all our sakes, my dear brother *Shandy*, do let this story of our aunt and her ashes sleep in peace. How can you have so little feeling and compassion for the character of our family?'

'What is the character of a family to an hypothesis,' was *Walter Shandy's* response, who sought to have an hypothesis for all aspects of life, especially so in relation to truth. The Captain did not seek to reply with any other kind of argument, but whistled half a dozen bars of Lillibullero. On the few occasions when he was driven to further argument, the manner in which the Captain laid down his pipe showed his intention.

One occasion I recollect when the Captain put down his pipe in this manner, was when his brother was engaged in philosophising about the unsatisfactory method of propagating the human race, and bewailing the fact that the passion it entailed often coupled wise men with fools. Mrs *Shandy* was present but, used to her husband's pontificating, gave no reaction to what could have been seen as directed at her. Mr *Shandy* also commented on the process of procreation generally taking place in darkness, and there being no acceptable words to describe the procedure. He went on to make the comparison with the treatment of the opposite function. 'The act of killing and destroying a man,' he said, turning to the Captain, 'you see, is glorious—and the weapons by which we do it, are honourable. We march with them upon our shoulders—we strut with them by our sides. We gild and carve them—' The Captain laid down his pipe in the particular way I recognised, and seemed about to challenge his brother when *Obadiah* came into the room with a complaint which required an immediate hearing.

'My cow has no calf,' *Obadiah* informed the gathering, agitation in his voice.

Walter Shandy, following an established custom, was obliged to keep a bull for the service of the Parish. During the preceding summer *Obadiah* had one day led his cow to the bull for this service. It was the day he was married to one of the housemaids, and when his wife gave birth *Obadiah* expected his cow to do the same. He had visited the cow regularly for six weeks without any sign of a calf, and his suspicions fell upon the bull.

'Most of the townsmen think that 'tis all the bull's fault—'

'But may not a cow be barren?' said Mr *Shandy*, turning to Dr *Slop*.

'It never happens,' said the Doctor, 'but *Obadiah's* wife may have given birth before her time. Prithee has the child hair upon his head?'

'It is as hairy as I am,' said *Obadiah*, who had not had a razor to his face for several weeks.

'So brother *Toby*, this poor bull of mine, who is as good a bull as ever pissed, and might have done for *Europa* herself in purer times.'

'Lord!' said Mrs *Shandy*, 'what is all this story about?'

'A Cock and a Bull,' said *Yorick*, 'and one of the best of its kind I ever heard.'

Chapter Sixteen

Tristram's writing style has many peculiarities and idiosyncrasies, and he writes with the abandon of one who has such a high opinion of himself that he feels at liberty to express himself in any manner he wishes. Even to the point, in his conceit, of informing the reader of his greatness.

As my life and opinions are likely to make some noise in the world, and, if I conjecture right, will take in all ranks, professions, and denominations of men whatever,—be no less read than the Pilgrim's Progress itself.

For my own part, I am resolved never to read any book but my own, as long as I live.

Tristram, in his dedication of the book *To the Right Honourable Mr PITT*, clearly reveals his attitude behind the writing of it.

Sir,

Never poor Wight of a Dedicator had less hopes from his Dedication, than I have from this of mine; for it is written in a bye corner of the kingdom, and in a retired thatch'd house, where I live in a constant endeavour to fence against the infirmities of ill health, and other evils of life, by mirth; being firmly persuaded that every time a man smiles,—but much more so, when he laughs, that it adds something to this Fragment of Life.

I humbly beg, Sir, that you will honour this book by taking it—(not under your Protection,—it must protect itself, but)—into the country with you; where, if I am told, it has made you smile, or can conceive it has beguiled you of one moment's pain—I shall think myself as happy as a minister of state;—perhaps much happier than anyone (one only excepted) than I have ever read or heard of.

I am, great Sir,
(and what is more to your Honour,)
I am good Sir,

Your Well-Wisher,
and most humble Fellow-Subject
THE AUTHOR

There is here an early example of *Tristram* distorting the truth *(Shandy Hall)* had a roof of tiles) purely for effect. Several chapters into the book he even mocks the whole practice of dedications, producing a ready-made, all purpose dedication, which he offers for sale.

If therefore there is any one Duke, Marquis, Earl, Viscount, or Baron, who stands in need of a tight, genteel dedication, and whom the above will suit... it is much at his service for fifty guineas.

Be pleased, my good Lord, to order the sum to be paid into the hands of Mr Dodsley, for the benefit of the author, and in the next edition care shall be taken that this chapter be expunged, and your Lordship's titles, distinctions, arms and good actions, be placed at the front of the preceding chapter.

He later makes another real dedication preceding Volume V.

To the Right Honourable
JOHN,
Lord Viscount SPENCER

MY LORD,
I humbly beg leave to offer you these two Volumes; they are the best my talents, with such bad health as I have, could produce:—had providence granted me a larger stock of either, they had been a much more proper present to your Lordship.

I beg your Lordship will forgive me, if, at the same time I dedicate this work to you, I join LADY SPENCER, in the liberty I take of inscribing the story of Le Fever in the sixth volume to her name; for which I have no other motive, which my heart has informed me of, but that the story is a humane one.

I am,
My Lord,

Your Lordship's
Most devoted,
And most humble Servant.

In his book *Tristram* constantly digresses from the subject at hand, but he claims this to be an advantage of his writing.

Digressions, incontestably, are the sunshine;—they are the life, the soul of reading;—take them out of this book for instance,—you might as well take the book along with them.

This device of directly addressing the reader is frequently employed.

We'll not stop two moments, my dear Sir,—only as we have got thro' these five volumes (do, Sir, sit down upon a set—they are better than nothing) let us look back upon the country we have pass'd through.
—What a wilderness it has been! and what a mercy that we have both of us not been lost, or devoured by wild beasts in it.

*

I told the Christian reader—I say Christian—hoping he is one—and if he is not, I am sorry for it—and only beg he will consider the matter with himself, and not lay the blame entirely upon this book,—
I told him, Sir—for in good truth, when a man is telling a story in the strange way I do mine, he is obliged continually to be going backwards and forwards to keep tight together in the reader's fancy—which, for my own part, if I did not take heed to do more than at first, there is so much unfixed and equivocal matter starting up, with so many breaks and gaps in it,—and so little service do the stars afford, which, nevertheless, I hang up in some of the darkest passages, knowing that the world is apt to lose its way, with all the lights the sun itself at noon day can give it—and now, you see, I am lost myself;—
—But 'tis my father's fault, and whenever my brains come to be dissected, you will perceive, without spectacles, he has left a large uneven thread, as you sometimes see in an unsaleable piece of cambrick, running along the whole length of the web, and so untowardly, you cannot cut out

a **, (here I hang up a couple of lights again)—or a fillet, or a thumbstall, but it is seen or felt.—

Tristram does admit that in his writing he is sometimes at a loss for words, the right words, that is. He describes his particular answer to this problem, which is to shave off his beard.

Or that I am got, I know not how, into a cold unmetaphorical vein of infamous writing, and cannot take a plumb-lift out of it for my soul; so must be obliged to go on writing like a Dutch commentator to the end of the chapter, unless something be done—

—I never stand conferring with pen and ink for one moment; for if a pinch of snuff or a stride or two across the room will not do the business for me—I take a razor at once; and having tried the edge of it on the palm of my hand, without further ceremony, except that of first lathering my beard, I shave it off; taking care only if I do leave a hair, that it be not a grey one: this done, I change my shirt—put on a better coat—send for my last wig—put my topaz ring upon my finger; and in a word, dress myself from one end to the other of me, after my best fashion.

Now the devil in hell must be in it, if this does not do: for consider, Sir, as every man chuses to be present at the shaving of his own beard (though there is no rule without an exception) and unavoidably sits over himself the whole time it is doing, in case he has a hand in it—the Situation, like all others, has notions of her own to put into the brain—

There are occasions, I assume when he has already shaved off his beard, and his loss for words has re-occurred, that he resorts to several other means of expression. He avoids the delicate duty of describing widow *Wadman's* desirability by stooping to the device of leaving the page completely white in its blankness. It is the reader who is given the task of providing the missing description.

Let love therefore be what it will,—my uncle Toby fell into it.—And possibly, gentle reader, with such a temptation—so wouldst thou: For never did thy eyes behold, or thy concupiscence covet anything in this world more concupiscible than widow Wadman.

To conceive this right,—call for pen and ink—here's paper ready to your hand.—Sit down, Sir, paint her to your own mind—as like your mistress as you can—as unlike your wife as your conscience will let you—'tis all one to me—please put your own fancy in it.

Then comes the blank page, followed by this mocking comment from *Tristram:*

—Was ever anything in Nature so sweet!—so exquisite!—Then, dear Sir, how could my uncle Toby resist it?

Thrice happy book! thou wilt have one page, at least, within thy covers, which MALICE will not blacken, and which IGNORANCE cannot misrepresent.

Yet not content with using a blank page on the one occasion, he falls again into this slack way. In the Captain's announcement of his love, and when he and I enter widow *Wadman's* house, *Tristram* writes —*Let us go into the house*. But instead of the deserved description of events are two blank pages, supposedly to stir the imagination of the reader. Does the author wish the reader to take out quill and ink and fill up these pages also?

Throughout the book *Tristram* flaunts his learning, and he reproaches readers upon whom his numerous classical and learned references could be lost.

After citing various philosophers, including *Erasmus*, whose tracts on the subject of noses his father has acquired, *Tristram* mentions *Tickletoby's* mare.

—And pray who was Tickletoby's mare?—'tis just as discreditable and unscholar-like a question, Sir, as to have asked what year (ab. Urb.con.) the second Punic war broke out. —Who was Tickletoby's mare!— Read, read, read, read, my unlearned reader! read,—or by the knowledge of the great saint Paraleipomenon—I tell you before-hand, you had better throw down the book at once; for without much reading, by which your reverence knows, I mean much knowledge, you will no more be able to penetrate the moral of the next marbled page (motly emblem of my work!) than the world with all its sagacity has been able to unravel the

93

many opinions, transactions and truths which still lie mystically hid under the dark veil of the black one.

There follow two pages each bearing only a pattern of marbling.

There is perhaps some justification in the use of black pages as a substitute for a written expression of mourning. Two such pages are used to represent grief over the parson's death.

He lies buried in a corner of his church-yard, in the parish of——, under a plain marble slabb, which his friend Eugenius, by leave of his executors, laid upon his grave with no more than these three words of inscription serving both for his epitaph and elegy.

Alas, poor YORICK!

Ten times in a day has Yorick's ghost the consolation to hear his monumental inscription read over with such variety of plaintiff tones, as denote a general pity and esteem for him;—a footway crossing the church yard close by the side of his grave,—not a passenger goes by without stopping to cast a look up on it,—and sighing as he walks on, Alas, poor Yorick!

Then come the two totally black pages.

I am used directly as an aspect of another of *Tristram's* wandering from the use of words. Drawn on the page within an account of the Captain and I approaching Mrs *Wadman's* house, is a squiggly black line, said to illustrate the way in which I flourished my stick. *Tristram* describes it thus:

A thousand of my father's most subtle syllogisms could not have said more for celibacy,

In another chapter squiggly lines are drawn across the page, *Tristram* explaining that each one relates to his idea of the progression of the narrative in the previous volumes of the book.

These were the four lines I moved in through my first, second, third, and fourth volumes.—In the fifth volume I have been very good,—the precise line I have described in it being this:

There follows another, and less squiggly line.

By which it appears, that except for the curve, marked A where I took a trip to Navarre,—and the indented curve B, which is the short airing when I was there with Lady Baussiere and her page,--I have not taken the least frisk of a digression, till John le la Casse's devils led me the round you see marked D.

The extreme example of *Tristram* trying to make a point without using words, is his attempt to create the impression of a void. Chapter 23 is followed by Chapter 25; there is no Chapter 24.

—No doubt, Sir—there is a whole chapter wanting here—and a chasm of ten pages made in the book by it—but the book-binder is neither a knave, or a fool, or a puppy—nor is the book a jot more imperfect,(at least not on that score)—but on the contrary, the book is more perfect and complete by wanting the chapter, than having it.

Tristram's manner of writing, its peculiarities, idiosyncrasies, and general waywardness, shew that his purpose is to provoke humour, and in a manner which often apes his hero, *Cervantes*. In this wanton pursuit, truth, and my character, become casualties. Can such an author be given serious consideration, or credence, for the contents, descriptions and opinions expressed in his book?

95

10

Alan was on his way to Terry's local. He had been in the habit of having a drink there with Terry one night most weeks, though this had become less regular and he hadn't seen his friend for a couple of weeks. Their friendship had been established when they worked together. They now had little in common, Terry, divorced and living alone, full of complaints about his life, was becoming a depressing companion. Alan maintained contact from force of habit and, increasingly, from a feeling of obligation to his former comrade. He was beginning to prefer the company of Corporal Trim, someone Terry knew nothing of.

Expecting another dismal session, he was surprised to find Terry in an unusually cheery mood. He wondered what had happened to have brought about this liveliness; had a woman come into his life?

'I'm looking for contributions,' Terry said, when they were settled with their beers.

'Contributions?'

His friend produced a leaflet which had a photograph of a group of men holding up placards— OVERTURN THESE UNJUST CONVICTIONS written on them. 'It's a campaign to finally get justice for the men sent to prison for picketing— it was that big strike back in the seventies.'

Terry had been the union rep when they worked on the rigs. Alan had never been much of a union man until the accident, when it was the union which fought for proper compensation. 'I'm collecting for the campaign,' said Terry. 'I've been in touch with men I used to know in the building trade—£53 so far. Take some of these leaflets.'

Another photograph was of the men who had been sent to prison; one of them had the same name as Alan, and seeing it set his heart racing—could that be his dad?

'This man,' he said, his voice tight with the effort to control the rush of feeling, 'do you know anything about him?'

'Only what I've read here—are you thinking you might be related? I can make some enquiries.'

Too agitated to enjoy his beer, Alan declined another, gave Terry £2 for the campaign, and hurried home. The possibility that the man in the photograph might be his father filled his mind. He had only a vague memory of his dad who moved away from the family home when Alan was still a toddler. He never saw him again, his idea of the man moulded by his mother's bitter attitude to her former husband. Hints from others that his father had been sent to prison, had Alan growing up thinking his dad was a criminal; someone he didn't want to know about. But now his mind was bursting to find out more. Was his dad like Lilburne, locked up for being an agitator?

When he got to the flat he poured out his pent-up feelings to Wendy who, aware that there were closed areas in Alan's background, had never probed.

'You think this man might be your father?' she said, looking at a leaflet. 'There is a possible likeness.'

'I have to know,' said Alan, slumped in his chair.

'Your mother…?'

His mother had moved to Australia several years ago to be near her younger son, Jason, who had settled there. Wendy understood that Jason was the mother's favourite, and her preferential treatment of him the main reason for Alan leaving home and not continuing with his education.

'I'll write to her—she might tell me.' He would use the cottage address, let his mother know that her idol, Jason, was not the only one making headway in the world.

'There must be someone involved in the campaign who knows about this man,' said Wendy.

'There's a lot on the web about the campaign—here have a look.' It was the following evening.

He sat with the laptop, and quickly became engrossed in the history of the strike and the events which followed. It seemed to him that his father, if it was his father, had been a victim of collusion between the employers and a government intent on criminalising picketing. Alan read that at the earlier trial the defence made effective use of a right called peremptory challenge, and objected to any juror who was thought to have a business association with the construction industry. Shortly before the Shrewsbury trial the Lord Chancellor abolished this right. So even now, he thought, the rich and powerful were able to imprison someone agitating for fairer conditions—nearly four hundred years after John Lilburne was in the Tower.

Examples shown of headlines and reports appearing in the popular press depicted the strikers as being violent and threatening. Giving an image remarkably like the one Alan had grown up with of his father, though his mother had said nothing about a strike, or his dad being a picket. There was an email address and he sent off a request for information about the man with the same name. He also wrote to his mother, enclosing one of the leaflets, and asked her if the man was his father. The reply to his email came quickly, bringing the shattering news that the man was one of those who had since died.

'Dead… he's dead,' he said, limply.

'Your dad would have been quite an age by now,' said Wendy.

The other information was mainly about the man's union activities, and nothing about his personal background to suggest he was Alan's father. He sent another email, explaining the reason for his enquiry. This was acknowledged with a promise to see what more could be found.

He had difficulty in settling to anything whilst waiting to hear something that would end the uncertainty about the man who shared his name. In the cottage he would find himself staring out of the window, the drill silent in his hand. He couldn't concentrate on 'The Corporal's Story,' the page held unseen before him.

'You want him to be your dad, but the names might just be coincidence,' Wendy warned.

'I'm trying not to think of him as my dad…'

'…And there's no longer the possibility of any reunion.'

'It would be a kind of reunion for me—filling a gap in my life.'

A phone call came from one of the strikers who had been imprisoned. He said he'd worked with the dead man who had spoken of his two sons, often expressing regret that he had lost contact with them. This was almost enough for Alan, and confirmation came in a letter from his mother who, along with glowing accounts of her Australian grandchildren, wrote; 'That's him alright.'

From villain to a hero like John Lilburne. His father was transformed —a modern day Leveller. Alan's first reaction was to want to find out more about him, of his life after leaving. But what might he find? That his father had another family after the one he left? That there were aspects of the man's life that would tarnish the image of hero? And he was unlikely to discover any good reason for his father never having been in touch. He decided to do nothing.

The next time he met Terry at the pub, Alan pointed proudly to the man in the photograph on the leaflet.

'That's my dad,' he said.

Chapter Seventeen

A whole volume of *Tristram's* book is taken up with his hurried journey to *France*, undertaken in the belief that in this way he could avoid the death which he felt was threatening him. Yet it seems that for all his classical learning, he was unaware of the *Appointment in Samarra* legend. In this the servant of a *Bagdad* merchant is jostled in the marketplace by a woman he recognises as Death. She makes a threatening gesture to the servant, who flees from the market. He borrows the merchant's horse and rides many miles to *Samarra*, where he believes Death will not find him. The merchant goes to the market place and finds Death, asks her why she had threatened his servant. 'I was not threatening him,' she said, 'but showing surprise, for I have an appointment with him tonight in *Samarra*.'

In his desperate dash from Death, *Tristram never gave a peep into Rochester church, or took notice of the dock at Chatham, or visited St Thomas at Canterbury, though they all three laid in my way… I skip'd into the boat, and in five minutes we got under sail and scudded away like the wind.*

Pray captain, quoth I, as I was going down into the cabin, is a man never overtaken by Death in this passage?

Why, there is not time for a man to be sick in it, replied he—what a cursed liar! for I am sick as a horse… the wind chopp'd about!

He is a man in haste, travelling by post-chaise towards *Paris*, and thinking *that Death moreover might be nearer me than I imagined*, demanding that the horses be in the chaise exactly by four in the morning. From *Paris* he continues south, and in his account of *Auxerre* confuses the present visit with the much earlier one when on his grand tour. On that occasion he was accompanied by his father, unwilling to leave his son in the charge of any other person on this tour. The Captain and I,

Obadiah and several other members of the family were also part of the expedition. Though not Mrs *Shandy*, who was apparently taken up with the project of knitting her husband a pair of large worsted breeches, and had decided that she could be better occupied at home.

At *Auxerre* I went with the Captain and his brother to the abbey of *Saint Germain*, a visit recommended in some book Mr *Shandy* had been reading. He told the sacristan, a young brother of the order of Benedictines, that we wished to see the tombs of famous saints who had been lain to rest in the abbey. The sacristan lighted a torch, which was in the vestry for this purpose, and led us into the tomb of *St HeriBald*. This he told us, laying his hand on the tomb, was a renowned prince of the house of Bavaria, who under the reign of *Charlemagne*, had a great influence in the government, and had a principal hand in bringing everything into order and discipline.

'Then he must have been as great in the field,' said the Captain, 'as in the cabinet. I dare say he was a gallant soldier.'

'He was a monk,' said the sacristan, at which Mr *Shandy* slapped his thigh in delight, at this rebuff for his military brother.

'I shall return tomorrow to look at the other saints,' he said, now in the gayest humour.

'And while you are paying that visit, brother *Shandy*,' the Captain said, '*Trim* and I will mount the ramparts.'

Back in the present, still engaged in escaping from Death, and complaining of the slow travel, which he blames on the use in *France* of puny and ill-fed post-horses. *Tristram* arrives in *Lyons*, and decides to travel from there to *Avignon* by boat. Before he leaves, a commissary comes from the post office with a bill for the payment of several livres. Upon what account? he demands, and when told it is upon the part of the King, denies he owes the King of France nothing but his goodwill. You are indebted to him six livres and four sous, from hence to *St Fons* in your route to *Avignon*—which being a post royal, you pay double for the horses and postillion. *Tristram* explained that it was not his intention to take post but would be travelling on the river and had paid nine livres for his passage. His frustration increased when the commissary said that this made no difference, as he could chuse to take post if he wished.

Tristram swore that rather than pay for both the way he would go and the way he would not go, he would go to ten thousand Bastilles first. He continues his journey by boat, but does not say how the matter of his debt to the King of France was settled.

*

I had now the whole south of France, from the banks of the Rhône to those of Garonnes to traverse upon my mule at my own leisure—at my own leisure—for I had left Death, the lord knows—and He only—how far behind me.

The influence of his idol, *Cervantes*, lies heavily on this section of *Tristram's* book. In a semblance of *Don Quixote*, he takes to the saddle, though his *Rosinante* is a mule, and *Sancho Pancha* a man with a long gun on his back, striding ahead on foot. He asserts that he could have spent a month in *Pall Mall* without having so many adventures as on this journey, though these are nowhere much described, apart from one dalliance of this travelling English gentleman.

A sun-burnt daughter of Labour rose up from the groupe to meet me as I advanced towards them, her hair, which was a dark chestnut, approaching rather to black, was tied up in a knot, all but a single tress.

We want a cavalier, said she, holding out both her hands, as if to offer them—And a cavalier ye shall have, said I, taking hold of both of them.

Tristram gives the impression throughout that he is harbouring his experiences of travelling through France for publication in another book. He cuts short one story: *You will read the whole of it—not this year... but you will read it in the collection of those which have arose out of the journey across this plain.*

Chapter Eighteen

Mrs *Wadman*, in her seventh year of widowhood, and whose property ran alongside the Captain's, showed considerable interest when he arrived. She was delighted to offer, this eligible member of the *Shandy* family, accommodation in her home until the Captain's house could be made ready. He accepted this kindly gesture gratefully, as not being expected at the *Hall* he had faced the prospect of having to stay at the dismal village hostelry. It was from *Bridget*, with whom a friendship had taken hold during those few days under Mrs *Wadman's* roof, that I later learned of her mistress's strong attraction for the Captain. She told me that on the first night of the Captain's stay, as soon as he had gone up to bed her mistress sank into her arm chair and stayed up much later than usual. "Till midnight,' said *Bridget*, 'and seemed in deep thought.' On the second night the widow had out her marriage settlement to which she gave careful study. But it was the third, and last night of our stay, that had left the greater impression on *Bridget*.

'My mistress was in the habit of wearing a long shift in bed which, when she lay down, I doubled over her feet and fastened it back with a corking pin. I was about to do this as usual when she kicked the pin out of my hand leaving her feet free, and dismissed me for the night.

The Captain was completely unaware of the ferment he had brought about in Mrs *Wadman*. Her romantic feelings towards him continued undiminished, becoming readily apparent to the *Shandy* household, causing Mr *Shandy* to declare that when a woman had experienced the presence of a man within her home among her own goods and chattels, he quickly became included in her inventory. The one person who continued to remain ignorant of the effect he'd wrought upon his neighbour, was the Captain.

Her heart firmly set on the Captain, Mrs *Wadman* was not deterred by there being no sign yet of any returning interest. She prepared for a lengthy campaign, ready to take advantage of any favourable development which might occur. Within the thick yew hedge that separated the widow's garden from the Captain's, she had an arbour constructed. Unobserved from within this she could overhear conversations in the neighbouring garden, and she now sat there for hours listening intently for any illuminating expression of the Captain's thoughts on life and matrimony. 'If the Captain is out there you can be sure my mistress is at her post in the arbour,' *Bridget* said.

The widow's vigil had been rewarded with a wealth of information regarding military fortifications but almost no insight into the Captain's emotional state of mind. The conversations she became privy to limited almost entirely to the instructions that he, sitting with his plans in the sentry box, passed on to me to guide my shaping of the model of the required fortification. One exception, *Bridget* told me, was my discussion with the Captain over who had suffered the most painful wound. Mrs *Wadman's* attention immediately aroused when mention was made of his groin, causing her to unpin her mob cap at the chin and stand up, not wishing to miss anything that was said about this vital area of the Captain's anatomy. Though it was no secret that his wound had been to the groin, the extent of the damage had remained shrouded, now had come her chance to learn more.

'There is no part of the body where a wound occasions more intolerable anguish than upon the knee,' she heard me say.

'Except the groin,' countered the Captain. Unknowingly alerting the widow in her arbour.

'The knee must be most acute,' I maintained, 'having so many tendons and the like attached to it.'

'That is the very reason why the groin is infinitely more sensitive,' he said, and our dispute continued for some time without coming to any accepted conclusion. Neither was the listening widow any better informed, having heard nothing to dispel any concern she might have about the effects of the wounding.

Her next manoeuvre, through the mediation of *Bridget*, was to seek to have a wicker gate made in the boundary 'to enable her to extend her walks.' With his unsuspecting heart the Captain gave leave for such a gate. The widow was now able to carry on her approaches to the very door of the sentry box, and she lost no time in taking advantage of this ability. Stopping at the narrow doorway of the sentry box she enquired of the Captain the nature of the present activity.

"Tis the 1658 siege of *Dunkirk*,' he said, gesturing with his pipe towards the map hanging on the wall by him. 'The English Commonwealth army, in an alliance with the French agreed by *Cromwell*, were seeking to end the costly attacks of Spanish privateers operating from this *Spanish Netherlands'* port. The siege lasted for a month...' the Captain warming to the subject, by which time the widow had stretched her neck in towards the plan of *Dunkirk*, one foot now firmly planted over the threshold. 'The Spanish garrison aided by English Royalists, defending from behind established fortifications,' continued the Captain. 'Show me,' said Mrs *Wadman*, and he lifted up the bottom of the map. She reached out her hand to hold its edge in a way that their two hands were touching, as also, in the confined space of the sentry box, were now their nearer legs.

Having progressed so far, the widow expected to advance further in such warm proximity, yet there was not the least indication of the Captain having been diverted from the siege of *Dunkirk*. She finally withdrew from the sentry box enriched only by the knowledge that, after a fierce battle, *Dunkirk* had become an English possession. Mrs *Wadman* persisted and made several similar attempts, gazing unseeingly at plans of the fortifications of *European* towns, deafened by her heated blood to the Captain's accounts of sieges and descriptions of fortifications.

Sustenance was given to Mrs *Wadman's* undernourished hopes when she overheard me telling the Captain of my love for the Beguine nun. He listened intently to my description of the tender touch of her hands, softer than satin, as she massaged my wounded leg. When I said my passion rose to the highest pitch and I seized her hand, he quickly added, 'then thou clapped it to thy lips and made a speech.' It was his romantic interjection which revived the widow's expectations. As soon as the story of my amour was finished, and seeing me leave the bowling-green, Mrs *Wadman*, wishing to take full advantage of the emotional atmosphere that had been created, sallied forth from her arbour and through the wicket gate. On her way she realised that her previous approach would not suffice, being completely overshadowed by the impact of the Beguine.

'I am half distracted, Captain *Shandy*,' she said, as she came up to the sentry box, holding her cambric handkerchief to her left eye. 'A mote—or something—I know not what, has got into this eye of mine.' Saying this she edged in beside the Captain and squeezed herself down upon the corner of his bench. 'If you could look into it.' And with his innocence of heart he looked and looked into Mrs *Wadman's* shining eye, rubbed his own eyes and looked again.

'I can see nothing, madam, whatsoever in your eye.'

'It's not in the white,' she said.

He gazed into the dark pupil, into an eye full of gentle salutations, and soft responses; an eye offering comfort and companionship, a bosom to lean on and trust his cares to.

'I'm in love, *Trim*,' he said, when I returned.

'You showed no sign of it when I left but a short time ago.'

'Mrs *Wadman* has left a ball here,' said he, pointing to his breast.

'This morning it was a different part of your person causing you concern.' The Captain had told me of a painful blister caused by riding on a faulty saddle, trotting too hastily with his brother in an attempt to save a beautiful wood that the dean and chapter were intent on hewing down, to provide fuel for the poor, they said. The wood was in full view of the Captain's house and of singular service to him in his description of the battle of *Wynnendale*.

'The blister has burst,' he said.

He spoke as if the physical relief this gave was a manifestation of being in love.

Next day, the Captain, who had no experience of being in love, wished to discuss how he should proceed. 'She knows no more at present of it, *Trim*, than the child unborn.' Mrs *Wadman* had told it with all its circumstances to *Bridget*, twenty-four hours before, and was at that very moment sitting in council with her. Meanwhile the Captain and I discussed his forthcoming visit to the widow to announce his love.

'I wish I may but manage it right, but I declare, *Trim*, I would rather march up to the very edge of a trench.'

'A woman is quite a different thing,' I told him.

'I suppose so,' he said.

In the evening when we went to the *Hall* his brother's greeting was; 'Well my dear brother *Toby*, and how goes it with your ASSE?' One of *Walter Shandy's* many idiosyncrasies was to use this term to describe passion, apparently after reading of *Helarion* the hermit who, seeking to control desire by practicing flagellation, spoke of controlling the body's kicking. Likening this to the behaviour of an ass, *Walter Shandy* adopted the term 'asse' for any reference to passion, well aware of the several meanings it gave.

'My ass is much better,' said the Captain, thinking of the part where he'd had the blister.

It brought a laugh from Doctor *Slop*, and a 'bless us' from Mrs *Shandy*, which deterred her husband from any further mischief with his asse.

'Everybody says you are in love, brother,' said Mrs *Shandy*. 'We hope it is true.'

'I'm as much in love, I believe, as any man usually is.'

'And when did you know?'

'When the blister broke,' said the Captain.

It may have been this strange reply which later caused his brother to write the Captain a letter giving advice on love and love-making. But Mr *Shandy's* immediate response was to commence a discourse on the nature of love.

'The ancients agree, brother *Toby*, that there are two different and distinct kinds of love, according to the different parts which are affected by it—the Brain or the Liver. I think that when a man is in love, it behoves him a little to consider which of the two he has fallen into.'

'What signifies it, brother *Shandy*, which of the two it is, provided it will but make a man marry and love his wife, and get a few children.'

'A few children,' exclaimed Mr *Shandy*, in disbelief, and glancing at Mrs *Shandy*, who took a pinch of snuff. 'A few children—not that I should be sorry had'st thou a score —on the contrary I should rejoice—and be as kind, *Toby*, to every one of them as a father. Nay, moreover, so much do'st thou possess of the mill of human nature, and so little of its asperities—'tis piteous the world is not peopled by creatures which resemble thee; and would I an Asiatic monarch I would procure thee—provided it would not impair thy strength—the most beautiful women in my empire, and oblige thee, *nolens, volens,* to beget for me one subject every month.'

'I would not,' said the Captain, 'get a child, whether I would or no, to please the greatest prince on earth.'

'And it would be cruel in me, brother *Toby*, to compel thee. But I put the case to shew thee, that it is not the begetting of a child—in case thou should'st be able—but the system of Love and marriage thou goest upon, which I would set thee right in.'

'There is at least,' said parson *Yorick*, 'a great deal of reason and plain sense in Captain *Shandy's* opinion of love. And in all the ill-spent hours of my life reading many flourishing poets and rhetoricians, I was never able to extract so much.'

'I wish,' said Mr *Shandy*, 'you had read *Plato*, for there you would have learnt that there are two Loves.'

'I know there were two religions among the ancients,' said *Yorick*, 'one for the vulgar and another for the learned; but I think ONE LOVE might have served both of them very well.'

An argument then commenced between Mr *Shandy* and the parson, each citing authorities such as *Ficinus, Velasius, Jupiter, Dione*—names that meant little to me, or to the Captain, who said; 'Pray brother what has a man who believes in God to do with this?' But his interruption did not staunch the gathered flow of *Walter Shandy's* discourse.

'I think the procreation of children as beneficial to the world,' said the parson, when Mr *Shandy* had paused, 'as the finding out of longitude—'

'To be sure,' said Mrs *Shandy*, 'love keeps peace in the world—'

'In the house—my dear,' said her husband.

'—it replenishes the earth.'

'But it keeps heaven empty,' my dear.

''Tis Virginity,' cried Dr *Slop*, triumphantly, 'which fills paradise.'

*

It was during our discussions about preparations for the occasion of the Captain's formal announcement to Mrs *Wadman*, of his love, that he showed me this letter.

My dear brother Toby

What I am going to say to thee, is upon the nature of women, and of love making to them, and perhaps it is as well for thee—tho' not so well for me— that thou hast occasion for a letter of instruction on this head, and that I am able to write it to thee. Had it been the good pleasure of him who disposes of our lots—and thou no sufferer by the knowledge, I had been well content that thou should have dipp'd the pen this moment into the ink, instead of myself; but that not being the case—Mrs Shandy being now close besides me, preparing for bed—I have thrown together without order, and just as they have come into my mind, such hints and documents as I deem may be of use to thee; intending, in this, to give thee a token of my love; not doubting, my dear Toby, of the manner in which it will be accepted.

In the first place, with regard to all which concerns religion in the affair—though I perceive from a glow in my cheek, that I blush as I begin to speak to thee upon the subject, as well knowing, notwithstanding thy unaffected secrecy, how few of its offices thou neglectest—yet I would remind thee of one (during the continuance of thy courtship) in a particular manner, which I would not have omitted, and that is, never go forth upon the enterprise, whether it be in the morning or afternoon, without first recommending thyself to the protection of Almighty God, that he may defend thee from the evil one.

Shave the whole top of thy crown clean, once at least every four or five days, but oftener if convenient, lest in taking off thy wig before her, thro' absence of mind, she should be able to discover how much has been cut away by Time—how much by Trim.— T'were better to keep ideas of baldness out of her fancy.

Always carry it in thy mind, and act upon it as a sure maxim, Toby— 'That women are timid:' And 'tis well they are—else there would be no dealing with them.

Let not thy breeches be too tight, or hang too loose about thy thighs, like the trunk hose of our ancestors. A just medium prevents all conclusions.

Whatever thou hast to say, be it more or less, forget not to utter it in a soft tone of voice. Silence, and whatever approaches it, weaves dreams of midnight secrecy into the brain: For this cause, if thou canst help it, never throw down the tongs and poker.

Avoid all kinds of pleasantries and facetiousness in thy discourse with her, and do whatever lies in thy power at the same time, to keep from her all books and writings which tend thereto: there are some devotional tracts, which if thou canst entice her to read over—it will be well: but suffer her not to look into Rabelais, or Scarron, or Don Quixote—

—They are all books which excite laughter, and thou knowest, dear Toby, there is no passion so serious as lust.

Stick a pin in the bosom of thy shirt, before thou enterest her parlour.

And if thou art permitted to sit on the same sopha with her, and she gives thee occasion to lay thy hand upon hers—beware of taking it—thou can'st not lay thy hand upon hers; but she will feel the temper of thine. Leave that and as many other things as thou canst, quite undetermined, by so doing thou will have her curiosity on thy side; and if she is not conquer'd by that, and thy ASSE continues kicking, which there is great reason to suppose—Thou must begin, with first losing a few ounces of blood below the ears, according to the practice of the ancient Scythians who cured the most intemperate fits of the appetite by that means.

Avicenna, after this, is for having the part anointed with the syrrup of hellebore, using proper evacuations and purges—and I believe rightly. But thou must eat little or no goat's flesh, nor red deer—not even foal's flesh by any means, and carefully abstain—that is as much as thou canst, from peacocks, cranes, coots, didappers, and water-hens—

As for thy drink—I need not tell thee, it must be infusions of VERVAIN and the herb HANEA, of which Aelean relates such effects, but if thy stomach palls with it— discontinue it from time to time, taking cucumbers, melons, purslane, water-lillies, woodbine and lettice, instead of them.

There is nothing further for thee, which occurs to me at present—

—Unless the breaking out of a fresh war—so wishing everything, dear Toby, for the best,

I rest thy affectionate brother,

WALTER SHANDY

'I could not have imagined, *Trim*, that there was so much to consider in these matters,' said the Captain, emitting a sigh.

11

For the first time they were having a serious discussion about the future, prompted by the pressing need for a decision about the cottage.

'I can't afford to leave my job,' Wendy said. 'There's not likely to be work for me out there, and the few buses are no good for commuting.'

'I'd be able to run you in to the shop—there's always some kind of building work in the City.'

'I'd have to take out a mortgage on the flat—how much would be needed?'

'It depends on what I can get for "The Corporal's Story".'

'It's all so uncertain.'

'There's three choices,' he said, 'renting, selling, living there. For renting, costs could be cut on things like kitchen and bathroom fittings, and as long as it looks good, something similar for selling. But if I knew I was going to live with it, I'd want top quality.'

'That would be expensive.'

'Three or four thousand more than the basic stuff—fourteen thousand total, say, to finish the job.'

'Let's go for that—we'll then have all three possibilities. And we might be able to charge more rent, or get a higher price if we sell.'

'You're wasted in that wool shop,' he said.

The kitchen units Alan expected were not now being delivered until tomorrow. He finished what he was able to do that day and went out into the village. His days there had been spent at the cottage, and his knowledge of the village was limited to a local shop and the nearby pub. Now with time on his hands he decided to look round the rest of the place. Coming onto an unfamiliar road he saw before him a substantial building, a wooden sign hung near the doorway. Shandy Hall, Alan read. He stood gazing at the Hall, his excitement rising. Here in front of his eyes was confirmation of his belief that the papers from the cottage were a valuable find. Breaking off from the hypnotic hold of Shandy Hall, he hurried back to the cottage and jumped into the pickup, eager to tell Wendy what he had discovered.

'So the cottage must be where Trim and the Captain lived,' Wendy's eyes widening, 'and where Trim hid his story.'

'No question of it now.'

'Are you going to take the manuscript to Shandy Hall?'

'No—the family might claim it belongs to them. I'd thought of going to the University. Somebody there should be able to say what these papers are worth.'

'There's part of the University near the shop—we could ask there.'

'I've almost finished reading Trim's story.'

'I'm nearly at the end—just a few more pages.'

'Next week then—we'll go next week.'

Chapter Nineteen

I set about preparing the clothes the Captain would be wearing for the occasion of his announcement of love. His wardrobe was extremely limited, and the only formal attire was his dress uniform which, as he never went much further than the bowling-green, had lain in his campaign trunk for the past fifteen years. When he tried on the blue and gold tunic he found it very tight, but as it was laced at the back and sides, as was the mode in *King William's* reign, this was easily remedied. It was his great ramallie wig which gave me most trouble. Squeezed in the corner of the campaign trunk those many years I had difficulty in giving it proper shape, even though I set the curls in pipes the time was too short to produce any great effect. The taylor's work on the thin scarlet breeches had produced little improvement, but the Captain's wardrobe held no alternative. Yet his sweet look of goodness assimilated everything around him so sovereignly to itself, that even his tarnished gold-laced hat and huge cockade of flimsy taffeta became a serious object the moment he put it on.

For myself I wore lieutenant *Le Fever's* regimental coat, which had been passed on to me after his sad death, and I had on my Montero cap.

We set out at eleven o'clock in the morning, I three paces behind the Captain, me with my stick hanging from a loop on the wrist and the Captain carrying his cane like a pike. Several times he turned his head back towards me as if looking for encouragement.

He halted twenty paces short of the widow's door.

'She cannot, *Trim*, take it amiss?'

'She will take it,' I said, 'just as the Jew's widow at *Lisbon* took it of my brother *Tom*.' And I gave a distinctive flourish with my stick, which the Captain watched as if it were a wand. He looked closely at Mrs *Wadman's* house, and then earnestly towards his cottage and his bowling-green. He continued slowly forward, and I moved ahead, placing my hand on the door rapper as I awaited a signal from him. Within the house, *Bridget* said, her finger and thumb had been poised on the door latch, her mistress watching the approach from behind the window curtain of her bed-chamber. The door flew open before I had well given the rap, and the interval between it and the Captain's introduction into the parlour so short, that Mrs *Wadman* had just time to get from behind the curtain, lay a Bible on the table, and advance a step or two to receive him.

The Captain saluted Mrs *Wadman* after the manner in which women were saluted by men in the year of our Lord one thousand seven hundred and thirteen. He then sat down with her upon the sopha, and it was as he was sitting that, in three plain words, he announced his love for the widow. Mrs *Wadman* lowered her eyes modestly in expectation of hearing more, but the Captain had no talent for amplification, and having once told her that he loved her, left the matter to work after its own way. In the unexpected silence the widow's eyes became engaged in examination of the patterning on her dress. The silence becoming painful, she edged herself a little more towards him, blushing a little as she raised her eyes and initiated their discourse.

'The cares and disquietudes of the married state are very grave,' she said.

'I suppose so,' the Captain said.

'And when a man, such as you, Mr *Shandy*, so much at ease as you are, happy in yourself, with your friends and amusements—I wonder what reason can incline you to the state.'

'They are written in the *Common Prayer Book*,' said the Captain.

'Ah, children,' said Mrs *Wadman*, 'though a principle end perhaps of the institution, and the natural wish, I suppose of every parent, yet are there not certain sorrows and uncertain comforts. And what is there, dear sir, to compensate for the heartaches and disquieting apprehensions of a suffering and defenceless mother who brings them into life?'

'I declare, I know of none, unless it be the pleasure which it has pleased God.'

'Fiddlesticks,' she said.

The tone in which the widow uttered this word summoned up blood to the Captain's cheeks, feeling that he had got beyond his depth in this discussion, and he stopped short. He laid his hand on his heart and, without entering further into the pains and pleasures of matrimony, offered to take them as they were and share them along with her. He did not care to repeat his proposal of marriage, leaving it with her to work after its own way, as he had done with his declaration of love. Spying the Bible on the table, he took it up, and picking the passage of all others the most interesting to him, the siege of *Jericho*, he set himself to read it over. Never tiring of the story of how, on the seventh day, the city walls were brought down when the people shouted and the priests blew their trumpets.

Mrs *Wadman's* mind was busy with other matters of more pressing interest than a Biblical siege. The Captain expected that his proposal of marriage could alone be sufficient, but there was nothing in the nature of it to encourage it to work in a positive way, or to counter what had already been at work. It was no secret that the Captain's wound had been to the groin, but details of the damage remained shrouded. It was natural for Mrs *Wadman*, whose first husband was all his time afflicted with a sciatica, to wish to know the whereabouts of the wound, and how likely would it limit his ability to be the complete husband she desired. She had looked into books on anatomy but could make nothing of them. To clear up all she had asked Doctor *Slop*, 'if poor captain *Shandy* was ever likely to recover of his wound?'

'He is recovered,' the Doctor said.

'What! Quite?' she asked.

'Quite, madam.'

'But what do you mean by recovery?' She asked, but gained nothing further from the doctor.

'*Trim* is bound to have the complete picture,' she told *Bridget*, and pressed her to get the full details from her friend.

When *Bridget* tried to persuade me to reveal the private details of the Captain's wound, I resisted, and told her it would be a betrayal of trust. Mrs *Wadman* concluded that she would have to get the facts of his injury from the Captain himself. Sitting with him on the sopha she began her enquiries. Was it without remission—was it more tolerable in bed—could he lie on both sides alike with it—was he able to mount a horse? And similar questions leading around her central concern, uttered so tenderly and directed towards the Captain's heart, that he glowed under such solicitude.

'And whereabouts, dear Sir, did you receive this sad blow?' she said, glancing towards the waistband of the red plush breeches.

'I shall show you the very place,' he said, 'you shall lay your finger on it.'

Bridget told me that her mistress had been shocked by this answer, vowing to herself that she would not accept this suggestion. Her mind was still reeling when I was summoned to fetch the plans of the siege of *Namur*, on which the Captain could stick a pin in the actual spot among the fortifications where he had been struck down. The widow had no hesitation in placing her finger there.

I took the map back into the kitchen where *Bridget* was waiting, and spread it out before us upon the table. 'Here is the town of *Namur*', I said, one hand pointing it out to *Bridget* who was standing close by me, my other hand on her warm shoulder as she leaned forward to look. 'This is the cursed trench in which the Captain and I lay, and where he did receive the wound which crush'd him so miserably here,' showing her the place on myself.

'We thought it had been more in the middle,' she said.

'That would have undone us for ever,' I said.

'And left my poor mistress undone too.'

For reply I gave her a kiss.

The Captain presented himself at Mrs *Wadman's* each afternoon, sitting on the sopha and hearing much from the widow, but had little to communicate in return. At home one evening he laid down his pipe and began counting over to himself on his finger ends, all her perfections.

'Prithee, *Trim*,' he said, 'bring me a pen and ink.'

Which I did, and paper also. He picked up his pipe, and gestured me to sit close by him at the table.

'Take a full sheet—she has a thousand virtues.'

'Am I to set them down?' I asked.

'But they must be taken in their ranks, for of them all, the one which wins me most, and is security for the rest, is the compassionate and singular humanity of her character. I declare, that were I her brother, *Trim*, she could not make more constant and more tender enquiries about my sufferings.'

I said nothing, and wrote down 'Humanity' at the top of the page.

'How often,' said the Captain, 'does *Bridget* enquire after the wound on the cap of thy knee?'

'She never enquires after it at all,' I told him.

'That shews the difference in the character of the mistress and the maid. Had my wound been to the knee Mrs *Wadman* would have enquired into every circumstance relating to it a hundred times.'

'She would have enquired ten times as much about your groin,' I said.

'The pain, *Trim*, is equally excruciating, and compassion has as much to do with the one as the other.'

'God bless you, sir, what has a woman's compassion to do with a wound to a man's knee? Had your knee been shot into a thousand splinters, Mrs *Wadman* would have troubled her head as little about it as *Bridget*, because the knee is such a distance from the main body, whereas the groin, as you well know, is at the very core of a man.'

The Captain emitted a long, low whistle—but in a note which could scarce be heard across the table. He lay down his pipe as gently on the fender as if it had been spun from a spider's web.

'Let us go to my brother *Shandy*,' he said.

Chapter Twenty

The Captain resolved nevermore to venture into an entanglement with a woman, or to think of that sex, or aught associated with it. Without cause, or indeed desire, to adopt a similar attitude, my friendship with *Bridget* continued, although, following the Captain's withdrawal from his wooing of the widow, no longer meeting her in Mrs *Wadman's* kitchen. Therefore I did not let pass any opportunity that might allow us to spend some time together. The events of one of these occasions brought a deal of embarrassment.

The Captain was settled in his bed and, being my custom, I went outside to see that all was well with our fortifications. The model of *Dunkirk* still stood little changed, as we awaited news that the articles in the *Treaty of Utrecht* dealing with the demolition of its fortifications and harbour had finally taken place. With no other works in prospect on the bowling-green, the French prevarication was frustrating, causing the Captain and I to consider going ahead with our own interpretation of the Treaty requirements.

'Let us begin by making a breach in the ramparts, or main fortifications of the town,' I suggested.

'That will never do,' said the Captain, 'for in going that way the English garrison will not be safe in an hour, if the French are treacherous.'

'They can be as treacherous as devils,' I said.

'It gives me great concern when I hear it—for they don't want personal bravery. If a breach were made in the ramparts, they may enter it and make themselves masters of the place when they please.'

'Let them enter it if they dare,' I said, eager to get to work on our *Dunkirk*.

''Tis not,' the Captain said, holding his cane in a military manner, 'any part of the consideration of a commander, what the enemy dare—or what they dare not do. He must act with prudence. We will begin with the outworks, both towards the sea and the land. Then we'll demolish the mole—then fill up the harbour—then retire into the citadel, and blow it up into the air, and having done that, corporal, we'll embark for *England*.'

'We are there,' I said.

'Very true,' he said, looking at the church.

On this moon shining night I espied *Bridget* in the lane next to the bowling-green. Taking her by the hand, I led her among the fortifications, and in going too near the edge of a fossé slipped and fell backwards, and being linked arm in arm, pulled *Bridget* down with me. Our fall was against the model drawbridge, which shattered under our combined weight. I told the Captain the next morning, his concern taken up with thoughts of a replacement drawbridge, rather than the particular circumstances of its demolition.

Nothing in the village escapes notice, and from what leaked out of our accident, the gossips embroidered in a most scandalous manner. For days afterwards I had to endure much teasing about my moonlight escapade with *Bridget*, she too encountering the ribaldry of her friends.

The Captain occupied himself with the design of an improved drawbridge to replace the broken model. Yet he seemed in low spirits following the debacle with widow *Wadman*. Gone too was the excitement of post days on receiving the *Gazette*, reading a detailed account of the latest developments at a siege in *Marlborough's* campaign. Then, he holding the *Gazette*, and me carrying a spade, setting about breaking down, or building up the existing fortifications, to comply with the latest information. There had been periods when the *Flanders* mail was delayed by bad weather, and the Captain, and I too, had been gloomy. But we knew it would only be a matter of days before the strong westerly's in the

Channel abated. Now there was no campaign for the *Gazette* to report on.

I decided to put on a special show to lift the Captain's spirits and contrive a spectacle of a constant barrage from our model artillery. My poor brother *Tom*, of whom nothing had been heard now for many years, had sent along with the Montero cap, two Turkish tobacco pipes. These I joined to each of our six cannons by leather tubes, sealed with clay to the touch holes. The Turkish pipes were charged up with tobacco and lighted, and it was possible to produce puffs of smoke from the mouths of the cannons. I had worked through the night and everything was ready in the morning when the Captain arrived. He was delighted with my invention, blowing enthusiastically into the pipes, the smoking cannons giving a semblance of a constant barrage of artillery fire.

Yet his listlessness resumed, and he was spending less time at the fortifications. The Captain's wound began to suppurate, issuing a noxious discharge. I applied various foments which gave some relief from the increasing pain, but did not stem the ominous flow. The Captain again became confined to his bed, and I again his nurse. The difference now, apart from our closer friendship after many years together, was that in *London* there had been the hope and expectation of the wound being healed. The re-awakening of it left me with a feeling of foreboding.

Mr *Shandy* was greatly concerned by his brother's condition and, consulting his numerous herbal books, made a variety of suggestions about the composition of the poultices I used.

Dr *Slop* was called in, and several times examined the Captain's groin. He was pessimistic about the outcome, saying to Mr *Shandy* and I during one of his visits: 'These symptoms are a sign that the organism is relinquishing its hold on life.'

'We must confound the body's desire for death,' asserted *Walter Shandy*, shaken by the Doctor's diagnosis. 'And bring to bear on my brother the latest developments in medical science.'

He arranged a visit by one of the top medical men in the country, who examined the worsening Captain, and afterwards when asked his opinion, shook his head. I could conceive of no greater catastrophe than losing the Captain, and the prospect left me in despair.

'Do what you can, *Trim*, for my dear brother,' said Mr *Shandy*, 'I know he could be in no better hands.'

The Captain remained stoical in the face of his approaching death, displaying the bravery he showed when awaiting the onslaught of an advancing enemy. His fortitude helped quell my own fears when in his presence, and it was *Bridget* onto whom I released my feelings. 'I shall be with you,' she said, in an attempt to give me reassurance.

The Captain's condition worsened by the day. 'I see you and *Bridget* in this house, *Trim*,' he told me, his voice now almost a whisper. 'I have made provision for this to be possible.' Tears came to my eyes, and I could barely thank him without being overcome. One morning I found him lying silent, his face serene; life had departed quietly in the night. My tears flowed without restraint, my eyes still wet when I went to tell his brother. No hypothesis or philosophy in *Walter Shandy's* rational approach to matters of life and death, proved sufficient to curb the outpouring of grief with which he greeted my news. 'Oh *Toby*, in what corner of the world exists thy fellow?' he lamented, twice removing his spectacles to wipe his eyes.

Susannah returned to the house with me to help *Bridget* in the laying out of the Captain's body. The village joiner brought the coffin and, in his full regimental dress, we lay the Captain in it. I draped the room with black baize, and lit candles for the first of the nightly vigils. Each night I spent sitting in that candlelight, his brother, and also Mrs *Shandy*, sometimes joining me. On the day of the funeral, my hands shaking, I placed the Captain's sword and scabbard on the purple velvet pall, which was decorated with military ensigns. I took his mourning horse, as he had wished, by the bridle to follow the hearse to the church. Parson *Yorick* gave the funeral service, his touching oration leaving few unaffected in the crowded church. *Tristram Shandy*, whom I grant had much affection for his uncle *Toby*, looked particularly sorrowful.

At the graveside *Walter Shandy* cast in rosemary with an air of desolation which was like my own. I felt that, along with the Captain, my life had ended.

Chapter Twenty-One

Walter Shandy was not pleased to see me in occupation of the Captain's house, and his son denied the property he had expected to inherit from his uncle. When the Captain first told his brother that he intended to leave the house to me, and to make provision for me to receive a pension, he had almost exploded.

'What is this madness?' he demanded, flushed with anger.

'*Trim* has been a good and faithful companion.'

'That I grant you, brother, and deserving of some recognition. But this—for a servant? It is beyond all reason. I cannot think what effect it will have on servants. And how will it be received by our friends—a servant treated as if he were family?' His voice rising in indignation.

'I could not be at peace,' brother *Shandy*, 'without knowing that *Trim's* future was secure.'

'You are a *Shandy*—your first obligation is to the family.'

'My first obligation is to God and my conscience.'

In vain had his brother tried to dissuade the Captain from making the bequests, and now there was talk of the family contesting the will. This, and whatever else was happening at the *Hall*, I learned from *Susannah* and *Obadiah* who became my regular visitors. It seemed that unexpected support for me came from Mrs *Shandy*, who spoke against any attempt to go against her dead brother-in-law's intentions. And parson *Yorick* was of a similar view, advising against any legal challenge. Shunned by the *Shandy* family, and not yet feeling secure in the house, it was not until I received the legal documents authorising my possession of the property that I felt able to marry *Bridget*.

Our wedding took place in the house, there we made our vows before parson *Yorick*. *Bridget* had put on a white dress and was wearing my wedding gift, the necklace I had sent to her that morning. I wore the wedding shirt she had sewed for me. Mrs *Wadman*, who had got *Bridget* a pair of handsome shoes, was present to hear our wedding vows. *Obadiah* contrived to be there, but could not stay, he said, though he remained long enough to down a couple of glasses of the port I'd provided. We others drank port and ate the biscuits *Bridget* had baked. *Susannah* joined us later, rushing in all excited. 'Off you go, Mrs *Shandy* said, when I told her of the wedding. And take this blue ribbon for *Bridget*.'

Until *Bridget* moved in it had continued to be the Captain's house, his presence everywhere, and saddening my thoughts. Gradually, with a wife by my side, it became our home. But the bowling-green would always be the Captain's. I preserved and maintained the fortifications and artillery as they had existed on his last visit. Sometimes I would go and sit in the sentry box and memories of our time together would crowd in with me. 'This place is your memorial to the good Captain,' *Bridget* said, as she walked with me round the fortifications.

Bridget was a welcome visitor to her former mistress, and she called in on Mrs *Wadman* once or twice in the week. 'She misses my company,' said *Bridget*, 'her new maid is a poor thing.' The widow had acquired a copy of *Tristram's* book and spoke to *Bridget* of it. 'It's not a book I can get along with,' she said, 'here; take it—though *Trim's* not going like the way *Tristram* writes of him.'

Mrs *Wadman's* opinion of what my reaction to the book would be was borne out, but she would not know the depth of feeling it aroused. I read the book with a growing sense of anger at the demeaning distortions of my character. Angry too that he had not spared his uncle *Toby*, frequently portraying him as a figure of fun in a vain attempt to emulate the humour of *Cervantes*. I began on these pages soon after reading Mrs *Wadman's* copy of the book. Only in the writing of this, '*The Corporal's Story*', have I been able to exercise control over my inflamed emotions.

The End

12

Alan had put on his freshly cleaned, light grey suit, and Wendy was wearing her new green skirt.

'I'm not going there looking like a builder,' he said, when they were discussing their visit to the University.

He carried the precious pages in an impressive looking red folder Wendy had bought at Smiths. They approached the historic building that housed part of the University, uncertain which of the medieval doorways they should enter.

'I feel nervous,' said Wendy, as they paused, gazing around this unfamiliar place.

'There's a lot riding on this,' Alan said, patting the red folder.

One entrance appeared to be the most used, and they followed close behind some students going in. Wendy, looking up at the patterned ceiling of the entrance hall, could imagine the Shandy family living in a place like this. Alan's eyes searched for an enquiry desk, somewhere he could ask about getting the information he wanted. We've come in the wrong entrance, he thought, and turned towards the doorway, unwilling to go further into the unknown interior of the building. Stationary in this hallway of constant movement, their bewildered appearance attracted the attention of a woman carrying an armful of files.

'Do you need some help?' she asked.

'I wanted to talk to somebody about some old papers I found,' Alan said.

'A manuscript,' said Wendy.

'How old is it?'

'It was written in the seventeen hundreds,' Alan said.

'Well, you've come to the right place. It's where we do the MA in Eighteenth Century Studies.'

'It's in here,' he said, holding up the folder. 'Will you be able to tell us about it?'

'Not me—I'm admin, but I'm sure I will find someone who can. Come with me.'

They followed her into an office, where they sat listening as she spoke to someone on the phone.

'One of the lecturers will come and have word with you—says he'll be about fifteen minutes,' she said, when she put the phone down. 'You can wait here for him.'

'Thanks,' said Alan.

'You've been very kind,' Wendy said.

They looked at one another, sharing a growing feeling of excitement.

Alan took him for a student when he came into the office, but he proved to be the lecturer they were waiting for.

'The papers were behind some panelling in a cottage I'm doing up. They must have been there for years,' Alan told him.

'We'd like to know how important they are,' Wendy said.

Alan began to take the manuscript from the folder.

'I can't read it now—but I'll take it with me. It will be a good exercise for one of my students,' said the lecturer.

'It's a valuable document,' Alan said, looking alarmed.

'Not to worry, we are experienced in the care of ancient documents.'

'Perhaps we should have a receipt,' said Wendy.

'Of course,' and he wrote out a receipt on University headed paper. Wendy gave him their contact details, and the lecturer left with the red folder, promising to get in touch when the manuscript had been examined.

'I was expecting to learn something today,' said Alan, his voice flat.

'So was I,' said Wendy. 'We'll just have to wait.'

'It could be weeks—months if it's in the hands of some idle student.'

They went from the University in silence, Wendy back to the wool shop, and Alan to his parked pickup, then on to a builders merchant.

The following week Wendy received an email from Bernard Dewhurst, the lecturer who they had seen. He offered them an appointment in two days' time. 'This is it,' said Alan, his eyes bright with revived hope.

He went into the University building with more confidence than on the first visit. Wendy too, less overawed now that she had some familiarity with the place. She asked directions from a young woman who stood chatting with a group of other students, and was told that Dr Dewhurst's room was at the end of the corridor. Alan knocked on the partly open door. 'Come in,' came a voice. Dr Dewhurst was seated at a desk; he pointed them to two chairs. 'The Corporal's Story' lay on the desk next to the W H Smith folder. He turned to face them.

'This is a very unusual document,' he began. 'It is a fiction about a fiction.'

'What do you mean?' said Alan, anxiously.

'Tristram Shandy is a character in a novel written by Laurence Sterne. Corporal Trim, the Captain, widow Wadman, all the characters, are constructs, products of his imagination.'

'Oh dear,' sighed Wendy.

'But there's Shandy Hall—it's there in the village?' Alan's voice rising.

'What is now called Shandy Hall is where the author of "The Life and Opinions of Tristram Shandy", lived. When the Laurence Sterne Trust took it over they named the house Shandy Hall—to attract visitors I expect.'

Alan's insides hollowed, he felt sick. Wendy's face had gone white.

'It's an intriguing document,' Dr Dewhurst continued, the words lost to his stunned visitors.

'Not real people... there was no Corporal Trim,' Alan murmured in disbelief.

Wendy reached for his hand.

'The manuscript raises a number of intriguing questions,' said Dr Dewhurst. 'Who was the real author? What was the purpose in writing it? And critically, when was it written—is it contemporary with Sterne or a much later fabrication? I would be interested in finding the answers to these questions.'

'What, you want to buy these papers?' Wendy asked.

'On loan, perhaps—they have no intrinsic value.'

'What do think, Alan?' she said.

'I'd like to know who was behind this.' He felt emptied, something that had become important in his life had been taken from him.

'Anything we learn will be available to you,' said Dr Dewhurst. 'It will provide a suitable assignment for one of my students—checking for anachronisms in vocabulary and usage.'

Alan signed an agreement to loan 'The Corporal's Story' to the University, his signature spidery as he sought to control the tension in his hand. They left shortly afterwards, Wendy carrying the empty red folder.

'I feel like I've lost a friend—as if Corporal Trim has died,' he said.

'And the lovely Captain Toby gone too,' sighed Wendy.

'What are we going to do?' said Alan, without hope.

For two days now he had not been out to the cottage.

'I can't face it not being the home of Trim and the Captain,' he told Wendy.

'It's a sad blow,' she said.

'I feel cheated by this fellow Sterne.'

'We know nothing about him—maybe we should visit that Shandy Hall place.

'I don't know.'

'We should—and soon.'

Several days later Alan parked the pickup near to Shandy Hall.

'I feel I'm going into enemy territory—I don't like it.'

'Are you not curious?'

'Just a quick look round then.'

They emerged from Sterne's house more than an hour later, Wendy carrying a handful of leaflets. Alan drove along to the cottage and made a drink from tea bags he kept there, apologising for it being without milk, which had gone off.

'So Laurence Sterne was the parson here when he wrote his book,' said Wendy.

'It was turned down and he had to publish it at his own expense,' said Alan.

'Self-published—and the book became all the rage. A lot of it's about himself—nearly dying from tuberculosis, and going off to France to get away from the damp climate.'

'Death caught up with him back in England—not much older than me,' said Alan.

'I saw nothing about Trim's story at the Hall,' she said.

'Worthless—those papers. And I thought they were going to be the answer to my money worries.'

'I'm glad you found them—and that I've read "The Corporal's Story", whoever wrote it.'

'I can't imagine never having known Trim and the Captain.'

'Yes—and widow Wadman, Susannah, and the rest.'

Alan drained his tea. 'I was ready for something to drink. I could have done with a cuppa in there.'

'I'm surprised they don't do refreshments, with all the visitors they attract,' said Wendy, who had stood up and was looking out at the area at the back of the cottage. 'I still think of this house as the place where Trim and Bridget lived happily together.'

'And where Trim and the Captain built their fortifications out there,' said Alan.

'Do you know what I'm thinking?' she said.

'Yes.'

Epilogue

There were nine of them in her group, Mildred counted them as they came out of Shandy Hall; one was missing, the man of course, the only male on her U3A course. 'The Life and Opinions of Tristram Shandy' had been on the syllabus of the English Literature degree she had taken when she was young. She thought of those distant days with increasing nostalgia, and, although she had not opened the book since, the urge for some kind of re-connection with that carefree student time roused her to offer a course on 'The Life and Works of Laurence Sterne' to her fellow third-agers.

She had no trouble in recruiting people, or rather women, for the course. 'It's one of those books I've always thought I should read,' a common remark among them. One or two said they had attempted to read the book but hadn't got very far. Mildred was disapproving of anyone who did not finish a classic novel, though her attitude moderated significantly when she once again faced Sterne's convoluted structure, and became entangled in his wayward prose. She quickly decided that her course would concentrate more on the life of Laurence Sterne than on his works. She wondered what other places had sufficient associations with the author to justify further outings like today's.

Geoffrey now appeared, delayed she imagined, by having had to make another toilet visit. The need for frequent breaks was a feature of many U3A men, the age of the prostate, the thought, bringing a wry smile to Mildred's embattled face.

'Are you all right, Geoffrey? We're going for a drink and something to eat.'

Geoffrey nodded. She hoped he would be sparing in the amount of tea he drank; on the way here the minibus had to make a special stop for him, the journey less than twenty miles.

The group straggled through the village, passing the pub Mildred, who liked a tot at lunch-time, had first considered for their refreshment venue. Glad now that she had resisted that temptation; the minibus would have been stopping every few miles if Geoffrey had downed a couple of beers. Denied the immediate solace of alcohol, Mildred comforted herself by thinking of the large gin she would pour the minute she was home.

'It's called Uncle Toby's,' she told Sheila, who asked where they were going.

'Isn't he in the book?' said Sheila.

'Tristram's uncle,' said Geoffrey, 'Captain Shandy, who Corporal Trim is in service to.'

Well somebody's been reading Tristram Shandy, thought Mildred, perhaps he's worth the trouble of an extra comfort stop or two.

Mildred, who had a sweet tooth, had looked up Uncle Toby's on the web after an acquaintance had gone on about the lemon syllabub she'd eaten there. 'A visit to Uncle Toby's,' the website said, 'complements a visit to Shandy Hall. The opportunity at the Hall of imagining the life of Tristram Shandy extended to the two other important characters in Laurence Sterne's novel, Uncle Toby and Corporal Trim. With the additional advantage at Uncle Toby's of enjoying traditional home made food, tea brewed from the leaf, and freshly ground coffee.'

There were other things on the sample menu, as well as the syllabub, and which looked interesting, with plenty of choice for the vegetarians in her group. She had reserved tables for ten.

Arriving at Uncle Toby's, Mildred waited outside for the laggards to catch up before going in. The café was busier than she had expected, obviously attracting more than just people who were on a literary trail. Two tables had been placed together for her group. She chose traditional pease soup with freshly baked Bridget's Bread; most of the group deciding to have the same. The thick green soup had a tastiness beyond anything possible from peas alone, and the crusty wholemeal bread still had the warmth of the oven. But it was the pudding that stole the show for Mildred, Susannah's Lemon Syllabub, the best she had ever tasted. To drink she had a Shandy, a soft drink tasting of elderflowers.

Geoffrey, on his way back from the toilet, paused by a display of books and pamphlets about Laurence Sterne. 'There's one here called "Tristram Shandy Uncovered",' he announced, picking up a book. 'Could be a help in our study of Sterne's novel.'

'You get the gist of "Tristram Shandy", and it's a lot easier to follow,' said a man, at one of the other tables. 'I read it in a couple of days.' This immediately generated interest among members of the group.

The woman serving coffee paused and looked up, her gaze turned to where, out beyond the garden tables, by two ancient cannons, a man was painting a wooden sentry box. And she smiled.

*****